My Naughty Little Sister

A TREASURY
COLLECTION

Dedicated to naughty little sisters,
and their sisters, everywhere.

My Naughty Little Sister: 50th Anniversary Celebration first published in Great Britain 2002,
revised edition *My Naughty Little Sister: A Treasury Collection* published 2017 by Egmont Books Ltd
The Yellow Building, 1 Nicholas Road
London W11 4AN

Stories selected from *The Complete My Naughty Little Sister*
My Naughty Little Sister © 1952 Dorothy Edwards
More Naughty Little Sister Stories and Some Others © 1957, 1959
and 1970 Dorothy Edwards
My Naughty Little Sister's Friends © 1962 Dorothy Edwards
My Naughty Little Sister and Bad Harry © 1974 Dorothy Edwards
My Naughty Little Sister and Bad Harry's Rabbit © 1977 Dorothy Edwards

Illustrations copyright © 1968, 1969, 1970, 1974, 1977 Shirley Hughes
Colouring of the illustrations by Mark Burgess
Copyright © 1991, 1997 Egmont Books Ltd
Photograph of Shirley Hughes by Keith Hawkins

ISBN 978 1 4052 8449 3

65131/1

A CIP catalogue record for this book is available from The British Library

Printed and bound in the E.U.

My Naughty Little Sister

A TREASURY COLLECTION

DOROTHY EDWARDS

Illustrated by

Shirley Hughes

EGMONT

Contents

The author, and her naughty little sister

When My Naughty Little Sister was very young

The very first story   *2*

My Naughty Little Sister learns to talk   *6*

My Naughty Little Sister's toys   *12*

The bonfire pudding   *18*

My Naughty Little Sister and the ring   *26*

The Bad Harry stories

My Naughty Little Sister and Bad Harry   *34*

My Naughty Little Sister and Bad Harry at the library   *42*

My Naughty Little Sister at the party   *49*

My Naughty Little Sister and the workmen   *58*

Bad Harry's haircut   *66*

My Naughty Little Sister can be a good girl sometimes!

My Naughty Little Sister and the book-little-boy 72

My Naughty Little Sister and the big girl's bed 76

My Naughty Little Sister does knitting 82

The icy-cold tortoise 87

My Naughty Little Sister makes a bottle-tree 94

Naughty stories indeed!

Going fishing 102

Crusts 107

My Naughty Little Sister cuts out 113

When my father minded My Naughty Little Sister 120

My Naughty Little Sister is very sorry 128

The naughtiest story of all 136

The author, and her naughty little sister

Dorothy Violet Ellen Brown was born into a working-class family in Teddington, by the River Thames, on 6th November 1914. Her little sister, Phyllis (Phil), was born six years later.

Throughout her childhood, the young Dorothy experienced poverty and hardship in her own family as well as the world around her. Her father, Charlie, was a former stable-hand who volunteered for the army at the outbreak of the First World War. He was in France for most of the first four years of Dorothy's life, surviving the First Battle of Ypres and life in the trenches to become one of the millions who faced long periods of unemployment during the 1920s and 30s. But Dorothy's mother, Alice, came from a family of ten children who, along with Alice's parents, provided a loving environment for Dorothy and Phil.

Dorothy was a born raconteur. Her grandfather taught her to read and write, granting her full access to the tall, glass-fronted bookcase full of cheap and second-hand editions, that stood in his parlour. She wrote her very first story at the age of four – a piece she later described as 'exciting, horrifying and very misspelt' – and by the age of nineteen her poetry was in print. Throughout her twenties she published short stories, articles and verse for a variety of newspapers and literary magazines, including *Punch, The London Mystery Magazine, Argosy,* the *London Evening News* and *The Spectator.* Indeed, Dorothy was a compulsive writer who lived to tell stories. A devotee of M. R. James and Dorothy L. Sayers, she was particularly interested in ghost and mystery stories and had given little thought to writing for children.

In 1936, whilst working as catering manager for Odeon cinemas, she met Francis Edwards (Frank), a telephone engineer who shared her passion for literature, drama and music. They married in 1942 and went to live in Leigh village, Surrey, where their daughter Jane was born the following year. A son, Frank, was born in 1946 after they had moved to Reigate. It was a family holiday that saw the dawning of her most famous work, *My Naughty Little Sister.*

In 1950, Dorothy's family – Jane and the two Franks, and her sister Phil – had hired a car for the holidays. The gentleman who had leased it to them insisted on driving, fearful of his car coming to harm. During the holiday it rained incessantly, and Jane, bored and miserable, asked her mother to tell her a story. Dorothy invented a story which began, 'A long time ago when I was a little girl, I had a sister who was littler than me. My little sister had brown eyes, and red hair, and a pinkish nose, and she was very, very stubborn.' The story was about a disastrous fishing trip, during which the naughty little sister had got all her clothes wet after wading into the river to catch fish in her little basket – an event that had occurred during Dorothy and Phil's childhood in Teddington.

Jane asked for this story to be told over and over again that day, and all through the next day, so that the poor driver was driven to distraction! Dorothy knew that she had created a winning story . . . 'Going Fishing'.

Are you sitting comfortably? Then I'll begin!

So began BBC radio's *Listen With Mother*, every afternoon at 1.45pm; a fifteen-minute programme of stories, songs and nursery rhymes that had an audience of over one million at its peak. In 1951, early on in the show's life, the editor asked parents to write in with comments and suggestions. Dorothy wrote in saying she thought the programme was very good, but she felt the stories came across as being read. She had come from a rich working-class oral culture, where adults shared stories with their children through their telling, and believed that telling rather than reading engaged young minds.

With her letter, she included a sample story constructed with the sounds and intonations that would help the reader include the young listener and tell the tale. The story was of course 'Going fishing' – the words being just as the children wanted them by now because Jane and Frank knew it by heart. When 'Going Fishing' was broadcast, it was so popular that parents all over the country wrote letters to the editor requesting repeats.

Dorothy wrote a further thirteen stories, and in 1952 Methuen published the first collection, *My Naughty Little Sister – Stories From Listen With Mother*, which Dorothy dedicated 'For My Sister Phil'. The success of this

was followed by *More Naughty Little Sister Stories and some others*, in 1957, and *My Naughty Little Sister's Friends*, in 1962. The first three collections were illustrated by three different artists, but in 1968, Methuen commissioned Shirley Hughes to illustrate *When My Naughty Little Sister Was Good*.

The first edition, illustrated by Henrietta Garland, 1952.

Illustrated by Caroline Guthrie, 1957.

Illustrated by Una J. Place, 1962.

Shirley Hughes

PENCIL SKETCHES FOR 'MY NAUGHTY LITTLE SISTER' and 'BAD HARRY' characters
FROM STORIES BY DOROTHY EDWARDS

Shirley Hughes at the drawing board.

Shirley was already well-acquainted with the stories, having read them time and time again to her own children. Dorothy was so pleased with the illustrations that she asked Methuen to commission Shirley to illustrate the stories retrospectively, which established the visual image of *My Naughty Little Sister* that is familiar to so many generations of readers.

This was also quite a breakthrough for Shirley Hughes, who of course went on to write and illustrate over fifty books, winning major awards, receiving the OBE in 1999, and being made a Fellow of the Royal Society of Literature in 2000 for her contribution to children's literature.

Having run a company of actors with her husband, as well as an antique shop, and with her own family grown-up, Dorothy Edwards was now committed to writing for children. In 1969 she wrote *Tales of Joe and Timothy*, about two young lads living in a tall block of flats – Joe right at the top, and Timothy at the very bottom, in the basement, where he could only see the people's legs going by. Over the next thirteen years she produced an extensive range of work, including stories for *Playschool* and *Jackanory*, collections of poetry, modern-day fairy-tales and books for older children. She also gave lectures and did radio work on children's

writing. The last Naughty Little Sister collection, *My Naughty Little Sister and Bad Harry*, appeared in 1974.

Listen With Mother enjoyed lasting popularity, and for some time Dorothy was herself a producer of the show, but audiences diminished with the launch of television's *Watch With Mother* and the programme ended in 1982. However, Dorothy Edwards' five Naughty Little Sister collections have remained in print and are likewise treasured fifty years after the first publication.

> *Now, my naughty little sister was a fidgety child. She wouldn't sit down quietly to hear a story like you do, or play nicely with a toy, or draw pictures with a pencil – she just fidgeted and wriggled and grumbled all the time . . .*

The incredible draw of Dorothy's stories lay in her real understanding of childhood and in her ability to address a young audience. A natural story-teller and strongly influenced by E. Nesbit and Beatrix Potter, Dorothy aimed to capture her audience through the sounds and rhythms of language as well as the strength of the story.

She also insisted that it was the children who dragged the stories out of her, during her countless visits to schools and libraries throughout Britain. Such was her warmth and chattiness that she could hold an audience spellbound, inventing stories on the spot and adding to them each time she visited a new group of children, making changes according to their

Dorothy and a captive audience, at a junior school in Chester.

response – her aim being to make the stories exactly as *they* wanted them. Dorothy felt particularly rewarded by the correspondence she received from children all over the world. One of the thousands was from a little boy from Canada, who was bitterly angry about Naughty Little Sister biting Father Christmas – in 'The naughtiest story of all' – and felt that this should be redressed!

By letting young readers in on this naughty little girl's thought processes, Dorothy's stories allow them to feel that they have an unparalleled understanding of this particular brand of misbehaviour. Naughty Little Sister breaks all the little rules, but because she is so young she never suffers from any guilt, and to that end personifies a type of naughtiness that no one

could ever be too angry about. Naughty Little Sister is such a nice child at heart, always eager to put things right.

Dorothy's sister Phil died in 1977, and soon afterwards Dorothy realised that she was herself unwell. A devout Christian, she responded by continuing to create wonderful stories, including *A Strong and Willing Girl*, in 1980 – a vivid account based upon the life of Dorothy's Aunt Grace who had been a maidservant in a Victorian household – and *The Witches and the Grinnygog*, in 1982, which was adapted for television.

Dorothy died on 9th August 1982, and was buried next to her sister. In an obituary she was described as 'an active champion of the cause of children's reading . . . In particular, she campaigned against the "middle-class" image and appeal of books: she believed in books for all children.'

And for her fans, young and old, Dorothy Edwards will remain the

Dorothy in her garden in Reigate, 1968.

creator of a naughty little sister who, whether she is fidgeting or grumbling, refusing to eat her crusts or covering herself in trifle, hiding from fireworks or biting Father Christmas, throwing her sister's doll out of the window or paying a formal visit on Mrs Cocoa Jones, is at all times and unquestionably herself.

'I read the My Naughty Little Sister *stories with my children, and then, years later, with theirs – again and again and again, by request. I can still hear that pungent prose, which conjures up for me Dorothy herself – forthright, funny and astute.'*

PENELOPE LIVELY

'I cannot think of any child who would not delight in the awful behaviour of My Naughty Little Sister, *chiefly because they can laugh in a superior way at her spirited naughtiness while privately recognising their own. My memory of reading Dorothy's beautifully judged story to my own children – five, six, seven – is of conspiratorial nudges, winks and giggles. Of course they* would *never behave like that . . .'*

NINA BAWDEN

'Being commissioned to illustrate a collection of My Naughty Little Sister *stories, way back in 1968, was a wonderful break for me. Here at last was a character who came across so vividly that she materialised as soon as I put pencil to paper. Other books followed, and so did my friendship with Dorothy herself.'*

SHIRLEY HUGHES

'Universality in storytelling is something every writer aims for and few achieve. Dorothy's work had it as if by nature . . . The "chatty" nature of her writing gave the My Naughty Little Sister *books* their unique quality. The family atmosphere, the childish misunderstandings were those of any and every household. Her output was large and varied but these stories will always keep her name alive.'

ROBERT LEESON

'Dorothy looked like everyone's granny, but that didn't convey what an interesting woman she was. She had a deep knowledge of children and the world of books, and her experience included radio production, live theatre, antiques and the history of Punch and Judy. Above all she was a great storyteller. I shall never forget her fascinating phone calls, which would last at least three quarters of an hour.'

MARILYN MALIN

When My Naughty Little Sister was very young

*. . . before I'd even got indoors, I heard a
waily-waily noise coming from the house,
and my godmother-aunt said
'That is your new sister.'*

The very first story

A very long time ago, when I was a little girl, I didn't have a naughty little sister at all. I was a child all on my own. I had a father and a mother of course, but I hadn't any other little brothers or sisters – I was quite alone.

I was a very lucky little girl because I had a dear grannie and a dear grandad and lots of kind aunts and uncles to make a fuss of me. They played games with me, and gave me toys and took me for walks, and bought me ice-creams and told me stories, but I hadn't got a little sister.

Well now, one day, when I was a child on my own, I went to stay with my kind godmother-aunt in the country. My kind godmother-aunt was very good to me. She took me out every day to see the farm animals and to pick flowers, and she read stories to me, and let me cook little cakes and jam tarts in her oven, and I was very, very happy. I didn't want to go home one bit.

Then, one day, my godmother-aunt said, 'Here is a letter from your father, and what do you think he says?'

My aunt was smiling and smiling. 'What do you think he says?'

she asked. 'He says that you have a little baby sister waiting for you at home!'

I *was* excited! I said, 'I think I had better go home at once, don't you?' and my kind godmother-aunt said, 'I think you had indeed.' And she took me home that very day!

My aunt took me on a train and a bus and another bus, and then I was home!

And, do you know, before I'd even got indoors, I heard a waily-waily noise coming from the house, and my godmother-aunt said, 'That is your new sister.'

'Waah-waah,' my little sister was saying, 'waah-waah.'

I was surprised to think that such a very new child could make so much noise, and I ran straight indoors and straight upstairs and straight into my mother's bedroom. And there was my good kind mother sitting up in bed smiling and smiling, and there, in a cot that used to be my old cot, was my new cross little sister crying and crying!

3

My mother said, 'Sh-sh, baby, here is your big sister come to see you.' My mother lifted my naughty little baby sister out of the cot, and my little sister stopped crying at once.

My mother said, 'Come and look.'

My little sister was wrapped up in a big woolly white shawl, and my mother undid the shawl and there was my little sister! When my mother put her down on the bed, my little sister began to cry again.

She was a little, little red baby, crying and crying.

'Waah-waah, waah-waah,' – like that. Isn't it a nasty noise?

My little sister had tiny hands and tiny little feet. She went on crying and crying, and curling up her toes, and beating with her arms in a very cross way.

My mother said, 'She likes being lifted up and cuddled. She is a very good baby when she is being cuddled and fussed, but when I put her down she cries and cries. She is an artful pussy,' my mother said.

I was very sorry to see my little sister crying, and I was disappointed because I didn't want a crying little sister very much, but I went and looked at her. I looked at her little red face and her little screwed up eyes and her little crying mouth and then I said, 'Don't cry baby, don't cry, baby.'

And, do you know, when I said, 'Don't cry, baby,' my little sister *stopped crying*, really stopped crying at once. For me! Because *I* told her to. She opened her eyes and she looked and looked and she didn't cry any more.

My mother said, 'Just fancy! She must know you are her own big sister! She has stopped crying.'

I was pleased to think that my little sister had stopped crying because she knew I was her big sister, and I put my finger on my sister's tiny, tiny hand and my little sister caught hold of my finger tight with her little curly fingers.

My mother said I could hold my little sister on my lap if I was careful. So I sat down on a chair and my godmother-aunt put my little sister on to my lap, and I held her very carefully; and my little sister didn't cry at all. She went to sleep like a good baby.

And do you know, she was so small and so sweet and she held my finger so tightly with her little curly fingers that I loved her and loved her and although she often cried after that I never minded a bit, because I knew how nice and cuddly she could be when she was good!

My Naughty Little Sister
learns to talk

Once upon a time, when my sister and I were little children, we had a very nice next-door neighbour called Mrs Jones. Mrs Jones hadn't any children of her own, but she was very fond of my sister and me.

Mrs Jones especially liked my sister. Even when she was naughty! Even when she was a cross and naughty baby with a screamy red face, Mrs Jones would be kind and smiley to her, and say 'There's a duckie, then,' to her.

And sometimes Mrs Jones would be so kind and smiley that my bad little sister would forget to scream. She would stare at Mrs Jones instead, and when Mrs Jones said, 'Poor little thing, poor little thing,' to her, my sister would go all mousy quiet for her. My naughty little sister liked Mrs Jones.

When my sister was a very little baby girl, she couldn't talk at all at first. She just made funny, blowy, bubbly noises. But one day, without anyone telling her to, she said, 'Mum, Mum,' to our mother.

We were surprised. We told her she was a very clever baby. And because we were pleased she said, 'Mum, Mum,' again. And again. She said it and said it and said it until we got very used to it indeed.

Then another day when my sister was saying, 'Mum, Mum,' and playing with her piggy toes, she saw our father looking at her, so she said, 'Dad, Dad,' instead!

Father was very excited, and so was Mother, because our funny baby was saying 'Mum, Mum,' and 'Dad, Dad,' as well. I was excited too, and so was dear Mrs Jones.

And because we were so excited my sister went on and on, saying 'Dad, Dad, Dad,' and 'Mum, Mum, Mum,' over and over again until Father, Mother and I weren't a bit excited any more. Only dear Mrs Jones went on being specially pleased about it. She *was* a nice lady!

So, one morning, when Mrs Jones looked over the fence and saw my baby sister in her pram, sucking her finger, she said, 'Don't suck your finger, duckie. Say, "Dad, Dad," and "Mum, Mum," for Mrs Jones.'

And what do you think? My funny sister took her finger out of her mouth and said 'Doanes'. She said it very loudly, 'DOANES'– like that – and Mrs Jones was so astonished she dropped all her basket of wet washing.

'Doanes, Doanes, Doanes,' my sister said, because she couldn't

quite say 'Jones', and Mrs Jones was so pleased, she left all her wet
washing on the path, and ran in to fetch Mr Jones to come and hear.

Mr Jones, who had been hammering nails in the kitchen, came
out with a hammer in his hand and a nail in his mouth, running as
fast as he could to hear my sister say 'Doanes'.

When she said it to him too, Mr Jones said my sister was a 'little
knock-out', which meant she was very clever indeed.

After that my sister became their very special friend.

When she got bigger she started to say other words too, but
Mr and Mrs Jones still liked it best when she said 'Doanes' to them.
If she was in our garden and they were in their garden they always
talked to her. Even when she could walk and get into mischief they
still liked her.

One day a very funny thing happened. Mrs Jones was in her
kitchen washing a lettuce for Mr Jones's dinner when she heard
a little voice say 'Doanes' and there was my naughty little sister
standing on Mrs Jones's back door-step. AND NO ONE WAS
WITH HER.

And my little sister was smiling in a very pleased way.

The back gate was closed and the side gate was closed, and the
fence was so high she *couldn't* have got over it.

Mrs Jones was very pleased to see my sister, and gave her a big,

big kiss and a jam tart; but she was surprised as well, and said, 'How did you get here, duckie?'

But my little sister still didn't know enough words to tell about things. She just ate her jam tart, then she gave Mrs Jones a big kiss-with-jam-on, but she didn't say anything.

So Mrs Jones took my sister back to our house, and Mrs Jones and Mother wondered and wondered.

The very next day, when Mrs Jones was upstairs making her bed, she heard the little voice downstairs saying, 'Doanes, Doanes!' and there was my sister again!

And the back gate was shut, and the side gate was shut, and the fence was still too high for her to climb over.

Mrs Jones ran straight downstairs, and picked my sister up, and took her home again.

When Mr Jones came home, Mrs Jones told him, and Mother told Father, and they all stood in the gardens and talked. And my sister laughed but didn't say anything.

Then I remembered something I'd found out when I was only as big as my sister was then. Right up by a big bush at the back of our garden was a place in the fence where the wood wasn't nailed any more, and if you were little enough you could push the wood to the side and get through.

When I showed them the place, everybody laughed. My sister laughed very loud indeed, and then she went through the hole straight away to show how easy it was!

After that, my sister was always going in to see Mrs Jones, but because the hole was so small, and my sister was growing bigger

all the time, Mr Jones found another place in his fence, and he made a little gate there.

It was a dear little white gate, with an easy up and down handle. There was a step up to it, and a step down from it. Mr Jones planted a pink rose to go over the top of it, and made a path from the gate to his garden path.

All for my sister. It was her very own gate.

And when Mrs Jones knocked on our wall at eleven o'clock every morning, and my sister went in to have a cup of cocoa with her, she didn't have to go through a hole in the fence, she went through her very own COCOA JONES'S GATE.

My Naughty Little Sister's toys

Long ago, when my sister and I were little girls, we had a cousin called George who used to like making things with wood.

He made trays and boxes, and things with holes in to hang on the wall for pipes, and when he had made them he gave them away as presents.

George made me a chair for my Teddy-bear and a nice little bookcase for my story-books. Then George thought he would like to make something for my little sister.

Now that wasn't at all easy, because my sister was still a very little child. She still went out in a pram sometimes, she could walk a bit, but when she was in a great hurry she liked crawling better. She could say words though.

My sister had a very smart red pram. She liked her pram very much. She was always pleased when our mother took her out in it. She learned to say, 'pram, pram, pram,' when she saw it, and 'ride, ride, ride,' to show that she wanted to go out.

Well now, kind Cousin George was sorry to think that my sister liked crawling better than walking, so he said, 'I know, I will make her a little wooden horse-on-wheels so she can push herself along with it.'

And that is just what he did. He made a strong little wooden horse, with a long wavy tail, and a smiley-tooth face that he painted himself. He painted the horse white with black spots. Then he put strong red wheels on it, and a strong red handle.

It was a lovely pushing-horse.

I said, 'Oh, isn't it lovely?' and I pushed it up and down to show my sister. 'Look, baby, gee-gee,' I said.

My sister laughed. She was so glad to have the wooden horse. She stood up on her fat little legs and she got hold of the strong red handle, and she pushed too!

And when the horse ran away on his red wheels, my sister walked after him holding on to the red handle, and she walked, and WALKED. Clever Cousin George.

Mother said, 'That's a horse, dear. Say "Thank you, Cousin George, for the nice horse",' and she lifted my sister up so that she could give him a nice 'thank you' hug, because of course that was

13

the way my sister thanked people in those days.

Then Mother said, 'Horse, horse, horse,' so that my sister could learn the new word, and she patted the wooden horse when she said it.

But my sister didn't say 'Horse' at all. *She* patted the wooden horse too, but she said, 'Pram, pram, pram.'

And she picked up her tiny Teddy-bear, and she laid him on the pushing-horse's back, and she picked up my doll's cot blanket and covered Teddy up with it, and she pushed the horse up and down, and said, 'Pram.'

When George came to see us again, he was surprised to find that my funny little sister had made the horse into a pram, but he said, 'Well, anyway, she can walk now!' And so she could. She had stopped crawling.

Because George liked my little sister he made her another nice thing. He made her a pretty little doll's house, just big enough for her to play with. It had a room upstairs, and a room downstairs, and there were some pretty little chairs and a table and a bed in it that he had made himself.

When my sister saw this doll's house she smiled and smiled. When she opened the front of the doll's house and saw the things inside she smiled a lot more.

She took all the chairs and things out of the doll's house and laid them on the floor, and she began to play with it at once. But she didn't play houses with it at all.

Because there was a room upstairs and a room downstairs and a front that opened she said it was an oven! She pretended to light a light inside it, just as she had seen our mother do, when she was cooking the dinner, and she said, 'ov-en, ov-en.'

She called the chairs and table and the bed 'Dinner', and she put them back into the doll's house again, and pretended they were cooking, while she took tiny Teddy for a ride on the pushing-horse pram.

She played and played with her doll's house oven and her pushing-horse pram.

Our Cousin George said, 'What an extraordinary child you are.' Then he laughed. 'That gives me an idea!' he said.

And when he went away he was smiling to himself.

The next time George came he was still smiling, and when my sister saw what he had made she smiled too. This time she knew what it was.

George had made a lovely wooden pretending-stove with two ovens and a pretending fire, and a real tin chimney. We don't have stoves like these nowadays, but some people still did when I was young. There was one in our granny's house.

My sister said, 'Gran-gran oven,' at once.

I gave my little sister a toy saucepan and kettle from my toy box, and Mother gave her two little patty-tins.

George said, 'You can cook on the top, and in the ovens – just like Granny does.'

And that was just what my sister did do. She cooked pretending dinners on the wooden stove all day long, and Cousin George was very pleased to think she was playing in the right way with something he had made for her.

But that isn't the end of the story. Oh no.

One day my naughty little sister's bad friend Harry came to visit us with his mother. He was only a little baby boy then, but he liked playing with my sister even in those days.

When my little sister saw Harry, she said 'Boy-boy. Play oven.' She wanted Harry to cook dinners too.

Bad Harry looked at the wooden stove, and the real tin chimney and the pretending fire, and he said, 'Engine. Puff-puff.'

Then Harry pretended to put coal into the little fireplace. He

opened the oven doors and banged them
shut again just like the man who helped
the engine-driver did, and he made
choof-choof-choofy train noises.

Harry had been with his father to see
the trains and he knew just the right noises
to make and the right things to do.

My sister didn't know anything
about trains then, but it was such a
lovely game that she made all the
noises Harry made and said 'Engine' too.

After that she and Harry had lots of
lovely games playing engines with the little wooden stove.

When Cousin George heard about this, he said, 'Pram-horses
and oven-doll's houses, and now – engine-stoves!'

He said, 'It's no good. When that child is a bigger girl I shall just
give her some wood and some nails and let her make her own toys!'

I think he must have forgotten that he said this, because he never
did give her any wood and nails. I wonder what she would have
made if he had?

The bonfire pudding

When my sister was a little girl she didn't like Bonfire Night and fireworks. She didn't like them at all. I liked them very much and so did my sister's friend Harry, but she didn't.

She wouldn't even look out of the window on Bonfire Night.

She would say, 'It's burny and bangy, and I don't like it.'

So on Bonfire Nights, Mother stayed home with her, while our father took me out to let the fireworks off.

It was a pity because our mother *did* like fireworks.

Well now, one day, just before the Fifth of November (which is what Bonfire Night day is called) our mother took us round to our grandmother's house to pay a visit, and Mother told Granny all about my little sister not liking fireworks.

She said, 'It's such a pity, because this year the fireworks are going to be very grand. There is going to be a big bonfire on the common, and everyone is going there to let off fireworks.'

She said, 'There is going to be a Grand Opening with the Mayor, and a Band on a Lorry.'

Our mother said, 'I am sure she would like it. She likes music.'

But my sister looked very cross. She said, 'I do like music very much. But I don't like fireworks.'

Mother said, 'But they are going to have baked potatoes and sausages and spicy cakes and all sorts of nice things to eat.'

My sister said, 'I don't like bonfires.'

Mother said, 'You see, she is a stubborn child. She won't try to like them.'

But our granny wasn't a bit surprised. She said, 'Well, I don't like bonfires or fireworks either. I never did. I was always glad to get my children out of the house on the Fifth of November. It gave me a chance to do something much more interesting.

My little sister was glad to know that our grandmother didn't like fireworks either, so she went right up to Granny's chair and held her hand.

Granny said, 'You don't like fireworks and no more do I. Why don't you come and visit me on Firework Night? I think I can find something interesting for you to do.'

When Granny said this, she shut one of her eyes up, and made a funny face at my sister. She said, 'Why don't you come and have some fun with me? Then your mother can go to the common with your daddy and sister and have fun too.'

My sister made a funny face back at Granny, and said, 'Yes, I think I should like that.'

So on Bonfire Night, before it got too dark, Mother wrapped my little sister up in a warm coat and a big shawl and put her in a pushchair and hurried round to Grandmother's house.

She left my sister as soon as Granny opened the door, because she was in a hurry to get back.

'Come in,' said Granny to my little sister. 'You are just in time.' She helped my sister take her things off, and then she said, 'Now, into the kitchen, Missy.'

It was lovely and warm in the kitchen in our granny's house. My sister was very pleased to see the big fire and the black pussy asleep in front of it.

'Look,' said Granny. 'It's all ready.'

Granny's big kitchen table looked just like a shop, there were so many things on it. There were jars and bottles and packets, full of currants and sultanas and raisins and ginger and candied peel and a big heap of suet on a board, and a big heap of brown sugar on a plate. There were apples and oranges and lemons, and even some big clean carrots!

There was a big brown bowl standing on a chair that had a big, big, wooden spoon in it. And on the draining board were lots of white basins.

Can you guess? My sister couldn't. She didn't know what all this stuff was for, so Granny said, 'We are going to make the Family Christmas Puddings. I always make one for every one of my children every year. And I always make them on Bonfire Night. IT TAKES MY MIND OFF THE BANGS.'

My sister was very surprised to hear this, and to know that all these lovely things to eat were going to be made into Christmas Puddings.

Granny said, 'You can help me, and it will take your mind off the bangs, too.'

She said, 'I've looked out a little apron; it will just fit you. It used to belong to one of your aunties when she was a little girl.'

And she tied a nice white apron round my sister's little middle.

'Now,' Granny said, 'climb up to the sink, and wash and scrub your hands. They must be clean for cookery.'

So my sister climbed up to the sink and washed her hands, and Granny dried them for her, and then she was ready to help.

Granny found lots of things for her to do, and they laughed all the time.

Granny was quick as quick, and every time my sister finished doing one thing, she found something else for her to do at once.

Granny poured all the currants out on to the table and my sister looked to see if there were any stalky bits left in them. When she had done that, Granny told her to take the almonds out of the water, and pop them out of their brown skins. That was a lovely thing to do. When my sister popped an almond into her mouth Granny only laughed and said, 'I'll have one as well.'

Granny chopped the suet, then the almonds, and the ginger while my sister put the currants and sultanas and things into the big brown bowl for her. It was quite a hard job because she had to climb up and down so much, but she did it, and she didn't spill anything either. Granny was pleased.

Grandmother chopped the candied peel, and because my sister was so good and helpful she gave her one of the lovely, sugary, candied peel middles to suck.

While Granny crumbled bread and chopped apples and carrots,

she let my sister press the oranges and lemons in the squeezer.

All the time they chattered and laughed and never thought about Bonfire Night. They never noticed the bangs.

Once the black pussy jumped out of the chair and ran and hid himself under the dresser, but they were laughing so much they didn't even notice.

At the very end, Granny broke a lot of eggs into a basin; then she held the mixer while my sister turned the handle to beat them up.

And sometimes, while they were working, Granny would make a funny face at my sister, and eat a sultana, and sometimes my sister would make a funny face at Granny and eat a raisin!

When all the things had been put into the brown bowl, Granny began to mix and mix with the big spoon. She gave my sister a little wooden spoon so that she could mix too.

Then, Granny said, 'Now you must shut your eyes and stir, and make a wish. You always wish on a Christmas pudding mixture.'

And my sister did. She shut her eyes and turned her spoon round and round. Then Granny shut her eyes and wished.

My sister said, 'I wished I could come and help you next Bonfire Night, Granny.'

And Granny said, 'Well, Missy, that was just what I wished too!'

Then my sister sat quietly by the fire while our grandmother put the pudding mixture into all the basins, and covered them with paper and tied them with cloth.

My sister was very tired now, but she sat smiling and watching until Father came to fetch her.

Our father said, 'Goodness, Mother, do you still make the Christmas Puddings on Bonfire Night? Why, you used to when I was a boy.'

Granny said, 'This little girl and I think Bonfire Night is the best time of all for making Christmas puddings.'

She said, 'You may as well take your pudding now. It must be boiled all day tomorrow and again on Christmas Day. It should be extra good this year, as I had such a fine helper!'

So Father brought it home that night and on Christmas Day we had it for dinner.

My sister was so proud when she saw it going into the water on

Christmas morning she almost forgot her new toys.

And when we were sitting round the table, and Father poured brandy on it, and lit it, so that the pudding was covered with little blue flames, my sister said, 'Now it's a real bonfire pudding.'

My Naughty Little Sister
and the ring

A long time ago, when I was a little girl and my sister was a very, very little girl, she was always putting things into her mouth to see what they tasted like.

Even things that weren't meant to be tasted. And even though our mother had told her over and over again that it was a naughty thing to do.

Our mother would say, 'Look at that child! She's got something in her mouth *again!*'

She would pick my sister up and say, 'Now, now, Baby, give it to Mother.'

And my naughty little sister would take it out of her mouth and put it into Mother's hand.

My sister tasted all sorts of silly things; pennies, pencils, nails, pebbles – things like that.

Our mother said, 'One day you will swallow something like this, and then you *will* have a tummy-ache!'

But do you know, even though my sister didn't want to have a tummy-ache she *still* put things in her mouth!

Our mother said, 'It is a very *bad habit*.'

Well now, one day, a lady called Mrs Clarke came to tea with us. Mrs Clarke was very fond of children, and when she saw my little sister all neat and tidied up for the visit, she said, 'What a dear little girl.'

Now, my sister was quite a shy child, and sometimes when people came to our house she would hide behind our mother's skirt. But when Mrs Clarke said she was a dear little girl, and when she saw what a nice lady Mrs Clarke was, she smiled at her at once and went and sat on her lap when she asked her to.

Mrs Clarke played 'Ride a cock horse' with my little sister. Then she took my sister's fat little hand and played 'Round and round the garden' on it. Then she told my sister a funny little poem and made her laugh. My naughty little sister *did* like Mrs Clarke.

She liked her so much that when Mrs Clarke and our mother started talking to each other, she stayed on Mrs Clarke's lap and was as good as gold.

First my sister looked up at Mrs Clarke's nice powdery face. Then she twisted round and looked at the pretty flowers on Mrs Clarke's dress. There were some sparkly buttons on Mrs Clarke's dress too.

My sister touched all those sparkly buttons to see if they were hard or soft and then she turned again and looked at Mrs Clarke's hands.

When Mrs Clarke talked she waved and waved her hands, and my naughty little sister saw there was something very sparkly indeed on one of Mrs Clarke's fingers.

My sister said, 'Button. Pretty button,' and tried to get hold of it.

Our mother said, 'Why, she thinks it's one of your buttons!'

Mrs Clarke said, 'It's a ring dear. It's my diamond ring. Would you like to see it?' and she took the ring off her finger so that my little sister could hold it.

The diamond ring was very, very sparkly indeed. My little sister turned it and turned it, and lots of shiny lights came out of it in all directions. Sometimes the lights were white and sometimes they had colours in them. My sister couldn't stop looking at it.

Mrs Clarke said my sister could mind her ring for a little while, and then she and Mother started talking again.

Presently my little sister began to wonder if the ring would taste as sparkly as it looked. It was sparklier than fizzy lemonade. So of course she put the ring in her mouth, and of course it didn't taste like lemonade at all.

After that my sister listened to Mother and Mrs Clarke talking.

Mrs Clarke was a funny lady and she said things that made our mother laugh, and although my sister didn't know what she was laughing about, my sister began to laugh too, and Mrs Clarke hugged her and said she was a 'funny little duck'.

It was very nice until Mrs Clarke said, 'Well, I must think about going home soon,' because then she said, 'I'll have to have my ring back now, lovey.'

And the ring wasn't there.

It wasn't in my sister's hand. It wasn't on the table, or on the floor. *And it wasn't in my sister's mouth either.*

Our mother said, 'Did you put it in your mouth?' and she looked at my sister very hard.

And my sister said, in a tiny, tiny voice, 'Yes.'

Then our mother said, 'She must have swallowed it.' Mother looked so worried when she said this, that my sister got very frightened and began to scream.

She remembered what Mother had said about swallowing things that weren't meant to be eaten. She said, 'Oh! Oh! Tummy-ache! Tummy-ache!'

But Mrs Clarke said, 'It wouldn't be in your tummy yet, you know.' The sensible lady said, 'We'll take you along to the doctor's.'

But my sister went on crying and shouting, 'Swallowed it. Swallowed it.'

No one could stop her.

Then Father came home. When he heard the noise he was quite astonished. He shouted 'Quiet, quiet,' to my sister in such a bellowy voice that she stopped at once.

Then Father said, 'What's all the fuss about?' and our mother told him.

Father looked at my little sister, and then he looked at Mrs Clarke. He stared very hard at Mrs Clarke and then he laughed and laughed.

'Look,' he said, 'Look – look at Mrs Clarke's button.'

Mrs Clarke looked, Mother looked and even my frightened little sister looked, and there was the ring hanging on one of Mrs Clarke's shiny buttons!

My silly sister had taken it out of her mouth and hung it on to one of Mrs Clarke's dress-buttons to see which was the most glittery, and then she had forgotten all about it.

When our mother had said she must have swallowed it, my sister thought she really had.

She'd even thought she had a tummy-ache.

And she'd screamed and made a fuss.

What a silly child.

Father and Mother and Mrs Clarke laughed and laughed and laughed – they were so glad my naughty little sister hadn't swallowed the ring after all!

My sister didn't laugh though, she hid her face in Mother's lap and wouldn't come out again until Mrs Clarke had gone home.

But she never put anything in her mouth again – except the right things of course, like food and sweeties, and *toothbrushes*!

The Bad Harry stories

*You wouldn't think there could be another child
as naughty as my naughty little sister, would you?
But there was . . .
and this boy's name was Harry.*

My Naughty Little Sister and Bad Harry

Once upon a time – a long time ago – when I was a little girl, I had a sister who was littler than me. Now although my sister was sometimes very naughty she had a lot of friends. Some of her friends were grown-up people but some were quite young. Her favourite child-friend was a little boy called Harry. He often made my sister cross so she called him Bad Harry.

Bad Harry lived quite near to us. There were no roads to cross to get to his house, and he and my sister often went round to visit each other without any grown-up person having to take them.

One day, when my naughty little sister went round to Bad Harry's house it was his mother's washing day. Bad Harry was very pleased to see her; he didn't like it when his mother was doing washing.

'Have you come to play?' he asked.

Now Harry's mother didn't like naughty children running about in her house while she was doing the washing, so she said, 'You'll have to play in the garden then. You know what you two are like when there's water about!'

Harry said he didn't mind that. There was a lovely game they could play in the garden. They could play *Islands*.

There was a big heap of sand at the bottom of the garden that Harry's father was going to make a path with one day. Harry said, 'We'll pretend that sand is an island in the river, like the one we go to on the ferry-boat sometimes.'

My sister said, 'Yes. We will go and live on it. We will say that all the garden is the river.'

So off they went.

They had a good game pretending to live on the island. They filled Harry's toy truck with sand and ran it up and down the heap and tipped the sand over the island's side until it became quite flat.

35

Then they dug holes in the sand and stuck sticks in them and said they were planting trees.

Later on Harry went to find some more sticks and while he was gone my sister made sand-pies for their pretending dinner. My little sister made them in a flower-pot and tipped them out very carefully. They did look nice.

'Dinner time, Harry,' she said.

But instead of pretending to eat a sand-pie, that bad Bad Harry knocked all the pies over with a stick.

He said, 'Now you will have to make some more.'

He thought that was a funny thing to do. But my sister didn't think so.

My naughty little sister was very, very cross with Bad Harry when he knocked her pies over. She screamed and shouted and said, 'Get off my island, bad Bad Harry,' and she pushed him and he fell on to the garden.

When Harry fell my sister stopped being cross. She laughed instead. 'Now you're all wet in the river,' she said.

But Bad Harry didn't laugh. He was very angry.

'I'm not wet. I'm not wet,' he shouted, and he began to jump up and down. 'You pushed me. You pushed me,' Harry said.

'You broke my pies,' shouted my sister, 'Bad old Harry,' and *she* jumped up and down too.

Bad Harry was just going to shout again when he saw something and had an idea: he saw his mother's washing-basket.

Harry's mother had filled the washing-line with sheets and she'd left the other wet things in a basket on the path so that she could hang them up when the sheets were dry.

'I've got a boat,' Harry said.

He went up to the basket with the wet things in it.

'Look,' he said. 'It's a boat!' And he began to push it along the path.

My sister forgot about being cross with Harry because she liked his idea so much. She went to help him push.

'We've got a boat,' she said.

They pushed their boat round and round the island, and they were just talking about giving each other rides in it, on top of the wet washing, and my sister was just shouting again because she wanted to be first, when Harry's mother came out.

'You are naughty children,' Harry's mother said. 'If I hadn't caught you in time you would have got all my washing dirty. What will you do next?'

'We were playing Islands,' Bad Harry said.

'Well, you are not going to play Islands any more,' said Harry's

mother. 'You will come indoors with me where I can keep an eye on you!'

'Now,' she said. 'You can each sit on a chair while I wash the kitchen floor.'

She lifted Bad Harry on to one chair, and my naughty little sister on to another chair, and she said, 'Don't you *dare* get off!'

And they *didn't* dare get off. Harry's mother looked too cross. They didn't even talk – they were so busy watching her washing the floor.

First she used the mop on one corner. Then she picked up the chair with Bad Harry on it and put it on the wet place.

'There!' she said.

Then she washed the floor in another corner. She picked up the chair with my naughty little sister on it and put it on that wet place.

'There!' she said. 'Now don't get down till the floor is dry!'

She said, 'Curl your feet up and keep them out of the wet.'

And Bad Harry curled his feet, and my little sister curled her feet, and Bad Harry's mother laughed and said, 'Right, here I go!'

And she mopped all the floor that was left. She did it very, very quickly.

My little sister quite enjoyed watching Harry's mother mop the floor. She liked to see the mop going round and round and all the soap bubbles going round and round too. She liked to see it going backwards and forwards wiping up the bubbles. Every time the bubbles were wiped up she shouted, 'Gone away!' Our mother didn't clean *her* floor like that – so it was very interesting.

Bad Harry didn't shout though. He went very still and very quiet. He was thinking.

When Harry's mother was finished, she said, '*Well*, you *have* been good children. I'll just put some newspaper over the floor and you can get down.'

So she put newspaper all over the floor, and my little sister got down off her chair.

'Let's go and find a chocolate biscuit,' Harry's kind mother said.

My little sister smiled because she liked chocolate biscuits, but Bad Harry didn't smile. He didn't get down from his chair. He was still thinking.

He was pretending. All the time he had been on the chair he had been playing Islands. He had been pretending that the chair was an island and the wet floor was a river.

'Come on, Harry,' my naughty little sister said. 'Come and get your biscuit.'

'I can't. I'll fall in the river,' said Harry. 'I can't swim yet.'

My little sister knew at once that Harry had been playing.

She looked at the wet floor with the paper all over it, then she pulled the paper across the floor and laid it in a line from Harry's chair to the door. 'Come over the bridge,' she said.

And that's what he did. And after that they made up all sorts of games with newspapers on the floor.

My Naughty Little Sister and Bad Harry at the library

Nowadays libraries are very nice places where there are plenty of picture-books for children to look at, and a very nice lady who will let you take some home to read so long as you promise not to tear them or scribble in them.

When I was a little girl we had a library in the town where we lived. Our mother used to go there once a week to get a book to read, and when I was old enough I used to go with her to get a book for myself.

Our library wasn't as nice as the one nearest to your house. There wasn't a special children's part. The children's books were in a corner among the grown-up books, and all the books had dark brown library-covers – no nice bright picture-covers. You had to look inside them to find out what the stories were about.

Still, when I did look, I found some very good stories just as you do nowadays.

But we didn't have very nice people to give out the books.

There was a cross old man with glasses who didn't like children very much. When we brought our book back he would look through it very carefully to make sure we hadn't messed it up and grumble if he found a spot or a tear – even if it was nothing to do with us.

And there was a lady who used to say, 'Sh-sh-sh' all the time, and come and grumble if you held one book while you were looking at another one. She would say, 'All books to be returned to the shelves immediately.'

My little sister went to the library with us once, but she said she wouldn't come any more because she didn't like the shusshy lady and the glasses man. So after that Mrs Cocoa Jones minded her on library days.

So, you can imagine how surprised we were one day when she said, 'I want to go to the library.'

Our mother said, 'But you don't like the library. You're always saying how nasty it is there.'

But my little sister said, 'Yes, I do. I do like it *now*.'

She said, 'I don't want to go with you though, I want to go with Bad Harry's mother.'

What a surprise!

Our mother said, 'I don't suppose Harry's mother wants to take *you.* It must be hard enough for her with Harry.'

But, do you know, Harry's mother *did* want to take my sister. Bad Harry's mother said, '*Please* let her come with us. Harry has been worrying and worrying to ask you.'

So my mother said my little sister could go to the library with Bad Harry and his mother, but she said she thought she had better come along too.

'I don't trust those two bad children when they're together,' our mother said.

All the way to the library those naughty children walked in front of their mothers whispering and giggling together, and our mother said, 'I just hope they won't get up to mischief.'

But Harry's mother said, 'Oh no! *Harry is always as quiet as a mouse in the library.*'

Bad Harry – quiet as a mouse! Fancy that.

But so he was. And so was my sister. They were both as quiet as two mice.

When they got to the library, the man with glasses wasn't cross, he said 'Hello, sonny,' to Bad Harry and that was a surprise. (But of course at that time Harry still looked good.)

And then the shushing lady came along. She smiled at Harry, and Harry smiled at her, and the lady looked at my naughty little sister

and said, 'We don't mind good children like Harry coming here!'

My little sister was very surprised, and so was my mother, but Harry's mother said, 'Harry is always good in the library. He goes and sits in the little book-room in the corner, and he doesn't make a sound until I'm ready to go!'

Harry's mother said, 'He looks at the books on the table and he is as good as gold.'

Of course our mother was worried because she thought my sister couldn't be like that, but she let my sister go with Harry while she went to find herself a new book to read.

And, do you know, all the time our mother and Harry's mother were choosing books those children were quiet as mice.

And when our mother and Harry's mother were ready to go, there they were sitting good as gold, looking at a book in the little book-room.

When our mother got home she said, 'I would never have believed it. Those children were like *angels*!'

So after that my naughty little sister often went to the library with Bad Harry and his mother. And they were always quiet as mice.

Then one day Bad Harry's mother found out why.

One day when they were in the library she found a book very quickly, and, when she went along to the little book-room she had a great surprise. She couldn't see them anywhere!

Then she looked again, and there they were – under the book-table.

They were lying very still on their tummies, staring at something, and, as Harry's mother bent down to see what they were doing, a tiny mouse ran over the floor and into a hole in the wall!

You see, the very first time Harry had visited the library, he had seen that little mouse, and afterwards he always looked out for it.

He used to take things for it to eat sometimes: pieces of cheese and bacon-rind. The mouse had been Bad Harry's secret friend, and now it was my sister's secret friend too.

Harry's mother told our mother all about those funny children and the library mouse. She said, 'I suppose I ought to tell the librarian.'

But our mother said, 'I don't see why. That old man is always nibbling biscuits. He keeps them under the counter. He just encourages mice.'

I hadn't known about the biscuit nibbling, but the next time I went to get a book I peeped, and Mother was right. There was a bag of biscuits under the cross man's counter and piles of biscuit crumbs!

No wonder there was a library mouse. And no wonder it made friends with Bad Harry. The cheese and bacon bits must have been a great change from biscuit crumbs, musn't they?

My Naughty Little Sister
at the party

You wouldn't think there could be another child as naughty as my naughty little sister, would you? But there was. There was a thoroughly bad boy who was my naughty little sister's best boy-friend, and this boy's name was Harry.

This Bad Harry and my naughty little sister used to play together quite a lot in Harry's garden, or in our garden, and got up to dreadful mischief between them, picking all the baby gooseberries, and the green blackcurrants, and throwing sand on the flower-beds, and digging up the runner-bean seeds, and all the naughty sorts of things you never, never do in the garden.

Now, one day this Bad Harry's birthday was near, and Bad Harry's mother said he could have a birthday-party and invite lots of children to tea. So Bad Harry came round to our house with a pretty card in an envelope for my naughty little sister, and this card was an invitation asking my naughty little sister to come to the birthday-party.

Bad Harry told my naughty little sister that there would be a lovely tea with jellies and sandwiches and birthday-cake, and my naughty little sister said, 'Jolly good.'

And every time she thought about the party she said, 'Nice tea and birthday-cake.' Wasn't she greedy? And when the party day came she didn't make any fuss when my mother dressed her in her new green party-dress, and her green party-shoes and her green hair-ribbon, and she didn't fidget and she didn't wriggle her head about when she was having her hair combed, she kept as still as still, because she was so pleased to think about the party, and when my mother said, 'Now, what must you say at the party?' my naughty little sister said, 'I must say "nice tea".'

But my mother said, 'No, no, that *would* be a greedy thing to say. You must say, "please" and "thank you" like a good polite child, at tea-time, and say "thank you very much for having me", when the party is over.'

And my naughty little sister said, 'All right, Mother, I promise.'

So, my mother took my naughty little sister to the party, and what do you think the silly little girl did as soon as she got there? She went up to Bad Harry's mother and she said very quickly, 'Please-and-thank-you, and thank-you-very-much-for-having-me,' all at once – just like that, before she forgot to be polite, and then she said, 'Now, may I have a lovely tea?'

Wasn't that rude and greedy? Bad Harry's mother said, 'I'm afraid you will have to wait until all the other children are here, but Harry will show you the tea-table if you like.'

Bad Harry looked very smart in a blue party suit, with white socks and shoes and a real man's haircut, and he said, 'Come on, I'll show you.'

So they went into the tea-room and there was the birthday-tea

spread out on the table. Bad Harry's mother had made red jellies
and yellow jellies, and blancmanges and biscuits and sandwiches
and cakes-with-cherries-on, and a big birthday-cake with white
icing on it and candles and 'Happy Birthday Harry' written on it.

My naughty little sister's eyes grew bigger and bigger, and Bad
Harry said, 'There's something else in the larder. It's going to be
a surprise treat, but you shall see it because you are my best
girl-friend.'

So Bad Harry took my naughty little sister out into the kitchen
and they took chairs and climbed up to the larder shelf – which is a

dangerous thing to do, and it would have been their own faults if they had fallen down – and Bad Harry showed my naughty little sister a lovely spongy trifle, covered with creamy stuff and with silver balls and jelly-sweets on top. And my naughty little sister stared more than ever because she liked spongy trifle better than jellies or blancmanges or biscuits or sandwiches or cakes-with-cherries-on, or even birthday-cake, so she said, 'For me.'

Bad Harry said, 'For me too,' because he liked spongy trifle best as well.

Then Bad Harry's mother called to them and said, 'Come along, the other children are arriving.'

So they went to say, 'How do you do!' to the other children, and then Bad Harry's mother said, 'I think we will have a few games now before tea – just until everyone has arrived.'

All the other children stood in a ring and Bad Harry's mother said, 'Ring O'Roses first, I think.' And all the nice party children said, 'Oh, we'd like that.'

But my naughty little sister said, 'No Ring O'Roses – nasty Ring O'Roses' – just like that, because she didn't like Ring O'Roses very much, and Bad Harry said, 'Silly game.' So Bad Harry and my naughty little sister stood and watched the others. The other children sang beautifully too, they sang:

Ring O'Ring O'Roses,
A pocket full of posies –
A-tishoo, a-tishoo, we all fall down.

And they all fell down and laughed, but Harry and my naughty little sister didn't laugh. They got tired of watching and they went for a little walk. Do you know where they went to?

Yes. To the larder. To take another look at the spongy trifle. They climbed up on to the chairs to look at it really properly. It was very pretty.

'Ring O'Ring O'Roses,' sang the good party children.

'Nice jelly-sweets,' said my naughty little sister. 'Nice silver balls,' and she looked at that terribly bad Harry and he looked at her.

'Take one,' said the naughty boy, and my naughty little sister did take one, she took a red jelly-sweet from the top of the trifle; and then Bad Harry took a green jelly-sweet; and then my naughty little sister took a yellow jelly-sweet and a silver ball, and then Bad Harry took three jelly-sweets, red, green and yellow, and six silver balls. One, two, three, four, five, six, and put them all in his mouth at once.

Now some of the creamy stuff had come off on Bad Harry's finger and he liked it very much, so he put his finger into the creamy stuff on the trifle, and took some of it off and ate it, and my naughty little sister ate some too. I'm sorry to have to tell you this, because I feel so ashamed of them, and expect you feel ashamed of them too.

I hope you aren't too shocked to hear any more? Because, do you know, those two bad children forgot all about the party and the nice children all singing 'Ring O'Roses'. They took a spoon each and scraped off the creamy stuff and ate it, and then they began to eat the nice spongy inside.

Bad Harry said, 'Now we've made the trifle look so untidy, no one else will want any, so we may as well eat it all up.' So they dug away into the spongy inside of the trifle and found lots of nice fruit bits inside. It was a very big trifle, but those greedy children ate and ate.

Then, just as they had nearly finished the whole big trifle, the 'Ring O'Roses'-ing stopped, and Bad Harry's mother called, 'Where are you two? We are ready for tea.'

Then my naughty little sister was very frightened. Because she knew she had been very naughty, and she looked at Bad Harry and *he* knew *he* had been very naughty, and they both felt terrible. Bad Harry had a creamy mess of trifle all over his face, and even in his real man's haircut, and my naughty little sister had made her new green party-dress all trifly – you know how it happens if you eat too quickly and greedily.

'It's tea-time,' said Bad Harry, and he looked at my naughty little sister, and my naughty little sister thought of the jellies and the cakes and the sandwiches, and all the other things, and she felt very full of trifle, and she said, 'Don't want any.'

And do you know what she did? Just as Bad Harry's mother came into the kitchen, my naughty little sister slipped out of the door, and ran and ran all the way home. It was a good thing our home was only down the street and no roads to cross, or I don't know what would have happened to her.

Bad Harry's mother was so cross when she saw the trifle, that she sent Bad Harry straight to bed, and he had to stay there and hear all the nice children enjoying themselves.

I don't know what happened to him in the night, but I know my naughty little sister wasn't at all a well girl, from having eaten so much trifle – and I also know that she doesn't like spongy trifle any more.

My Naughty Little Sister
and the workmen

When my sister was a naughty little girl, she was a very, very inquisitive child. She was always looking and peeping into things that didn't belong to her. She used to open other people's cupboards and boxes just to find out what was inside.

Aren't you glad you aren't inquisitive like that?

Well now, one day a lot of workmen came to dig up all the roads near our house, and my little sister was very interested in them. They were very nice men, but some of them had rather loud shouty voices sometimes. They were shovelling men, and picking men, and men with jumping-about things that went *Ah-ah-ah-ah-ah-ah-aha-aaa,* and men who drank tea out of jam-pots, and men who cooked sausages over fires, and there was an old, old man who sat up all night when the other men had gone home, and who had a lot of coats and scarves to keep him warm.

There were lots of things for my little inquisitive sister to see, there were heaps of earth, and red lanterns for the old, old man to

light at night-time, and long pole-y things to keep people from falling down the holes in the road, and the workmen's huts, and many other things.

When the workmen were in our road, my little sister used to watch them every day. She used to lean over the gate and stare and stare, but when they went off to the next road she didn't see so much of them.

Well now, I will tell you about the inquisitive thing my naughty little sister did one day, shall I?

Yes. Well, do you remember Bad Harry who was my little sister's best boy-friend. Do you? I thought you did. Now this Bad Harry came one day to ask my mother if my little sister could go round to his house to play with him, and as Bad Harry's house wasn't far away, and as there were no roads to cross, my mother said my little sister could go.

So my little sister put on her hat and her coat, and her scarf and her gloves, because it was a cold nasty day, and went off with her best boy-friend to play with him.

They hurried along like good children until they came to the workmen in the next road, and then they went slow as slow, because there were so many things to see. They looked at this and at that, and when they got past the workmen they found a very curious thing.

By the road there was a tall hedge, and under the tall hedge there was a mackintoshy bundle.

Now this mackintoshy bundle hadn't anything to do with Bad Harry, and it hadn't anything to do with my naughty little sister, yet, do you know they were so inquisitive that they stopped and looked at it.

They had such a good look at it that they had to get right under the hedge to see, and when they got very near it they found it was an old mackintosh wrapped round something or other inside.

Weren't they naughty? They should have gone straight home to Bad Harry's mother's house, shouldn't they? But they didn't. They stayed and looked at the mackintoshy bundle.

And they opened it. They really truly did. It wasn't their bundle, but they opened it wide under the hedge, and do you know what was inside it? I know you aren't an inquisitive meddlesome child, but would you like to know?

Well, inside the bundle there were lots and lots of parcels and packages tied up in red handkerchiefs, and brown paper, and newspaper, and instead of putting them back again like nice children, those little horrors started to open all those parcels, and inside those parcels there were lots of things to eat!

There were sandwiches, and cakes and meat-pies and cold cooked fish, and eggs, and goodness knows what-all.

Weren't those bad children surprised? They couldn't think how all those sandwiches and things could have got into the old mackintosh.

Then Bad Harry said, 'Shall we eat some?' You remember he was a greedy lad. But my little sister said, 'No, it's picked-up-food.' My little sister knew that my mother had told her never, never to eat

picked-up food. You see she was good about *that*. Only she was very bad after that, because she said, 'I know, let's play with it.'

So they took out all those sandwiches and cakes and meat-pies and cold cooked fish and eggs, and they laid them out across the path and made them into pretty patterns on the ground. Then Bad Harry threw a sandwich at my little sister and she threw a meat-pie at him, and they began to have a lovely game.

And then, do you know what happened? A big roary voice called out, 'WHAT ARE YOU DOING WITH OUR DINNERS, YOU MONKEYS – YOU?' And there was a big workman coming towards them, looking so cross and angry that those two bad children screamed and screamed, and because the workman was so roary, they turned and ran and ran back down the road, and the big workman ran after them as cross as cross. Weren't they frightened?

When they got back to where the other road-men were digging, those children were more frightened than ever, because the big workman shouted to all the workmen all about what those naughty children had done with their dinners.

Yes, those poor workmen had put all their dinners under the hedge in the old mackintosh to keep them dry and safe until dinner-time. As well as being frightened, Bad Harry and my naughty little sister were very ashamed.

They were so ashamed that they did a most silly thing. When they heard the big workman telling the others about their dinners, those silly children ran and hid themselves in one of the pipes that the workmen were putting in the road.

My naughty little sister went first, and old Bad Harry after her. Because my naughty little sister was so frightened she wriggled in and in the pipe, and Bad Harry came wriggling after her, because he was frightened too.

And then a dreadful thing happened to my naughty little sister. That Bad Harry *stuck in the pipe* – and he couldn't get any farther. He was quite a round fat boy, you see, and he stuck fast as fast in the pipe.

Then didn't those sillies howl and howl.

My little sister howled because she didn't want to go on and on down the road-men's pipes on her own, and Bad Harry howled because he couldn't move at all.

It was all terrible of course, but the roary workman rescued them very quickly. He couldn't reach Bad Harry with his arm, but he got a long hooky iron thing, and he hooked it in Bad Harry's belt, and he pulled and pulled, and presently he pulled Bad Harry out of the pipe. Wasn't it a good thing they had the hooky iron? And wasn't it a good thing that Bad Harry had a strong belt on his coat?

When Bad Harry was out, my little sister wriggled back and back, and came out too, and when she saw all the poor workmen who wouldn't have any dinner, she cried and cried, and she told them what a sorry girl she was. She told the workmen that she and Bad

Harry hadn't known the mackintoshy bundle was their dinners, and Bad Harry said he was sorry too, and they were so really truly ashamed that the big workman said, 'Well, never mind this time. It's pay-day today, so we can all send the boy for fish and chips instead.' And he told my little sister not to cry any more.

So my little sister stopped crying, and she and Bad Harry both said they would never, never meddle and be inquisitive again.

Bad Harry's haircut

Quite a long time ago, when I was a little girl, my naughty little sister used to play with a little boy called Harry.

This boy Harry only lived a little way away from us, and as there were no nasty roads to cross between our houses, Harry used to come all on his own to play with my little sister, and she used to go all on her own to play with him. And they were Very Good Friends.

And they were both very naughty children. Oh dear!

But, if you could have seen this Bad Harry you wouldn't have said that he was a naughty child. He looked so very good. Yes, he looked very good indeed.

My little sister never looked very good, even when she was behaving herself, but Bad Harry looked good all the time.

My naughty little sister's friend Harry had big, big blue eyes and pretty golden curls like a baby angel, but oh dear, he was quite naughty all the same.

Now one day, when my little sister went round to play with Harry she found him looking very smart indeed. He was wearing real big boy's trousers. Real ones, with real big boy's buttons and real big boy's braces. Red braces like a very big boy! Wasn't he smart?

'Look,' said Bad Harry, 'look at my big boy's trousers.'

'Smart,' said my naughty little sister, 'smart boy.'

'I'm going to have a real boy's haircut too,' said Bad Harry. 'Today. Not Mummy with scissors any more; but a real boy's haircut in a real barber's shop!'

My word, he was a proud boy!

My little sister was *so* surprised, and Bad Harry was *so* pleased to see how surprised she was.

'I'll be a big boy then,' he said.

Then Harry's mother, who was a kind lady and liked my little sister very much, said that if she was a good girl she could come to the barber's and see Harry have his hair cut.

My little sister was so excited that she ran straight back home to tell our mother all about Harry's big boy's trousers and Harry's real boy's haircut. 'Can I go too, can I go too?' she asked our mother.

Our mother said, 'Yes, you may go, only hold very tight to Harry's

mother's hand when you cross the High Street,' and my sister
promised that she would hold very tight indeed.

So off they went to the barber's to get Harry a Real Boy's Haircut.

My little sister had never been in a barber's shop before and she
stared and stared. Bad Harry had never been in a barber's shop
either, but he didn't stare, he pretended that he knew all about it, he
picked up one of the barber's books and pretended to look at the
pictures in it, but he peeped all the time at the barber's shop.

There were three haircut-men in the barber's shop, and they
all had white coats and they all had black combs sticking out of
their pockets.

There were three white wash-basins with shiny taps and
looking-glasses, and three very funny chairs. In the three funny
chairs were three men all having something done to them by the
three haircut-men.

One man was having his hair cut with scissors, and one man
was having his neck clipped with clippers, and one man had a soapy
white face and he was being shaved!

And there were bottles and bottles, and brushes and brushes, and
towels and towels, and pretty pictures with writing on them, and all
sorts of things to see! My little sister looked and Bad Harry peeped
until it was Harry's turn to have his hair cut.

When it was Harry's turn one of the haircut-men fetched a
special high-chair for Harry to sit in, because the grown-up chairs
were all too big.

Harry sat in the special chair and then the haircut-man got a big
blue sheet and wrapped it round Harry and tucked it in at the neck.
'You don't want any tickly old hairs going down there,' the haircut-
man said.

Then the haircut-man took his sharp shiny scissors and began
to cut and cut. And down fell a golden curl and 'Gone!' said my little
sister, and down fell another golden curl and 'Gone!' said my little
sister again, and she said, 'Gone!' 'Gone!' 'Gone!' all the time until
Harry's curls had quite gone away.
Then she said, 'All gone now!'

When the haircut-man had
finished cutting he took a
bottle with a squeezer-
thing and he squirted
some nice smelly stuff
all over Harry's head,
and made Harry
laugh, and my little
sister laughed as well.

Then the haircut-man took the big black comb, and he made a Big Boy's Parting on Harry's head, and he combed Harry's hair back into a real boy's haircut and then Bad Harry climbed down from the high-chair so that my little sister could really look at him.

And then my little sister *did* stare. Bad Harry's mother stared too . . .

For there was that bad boy Harry, with his real boy's trousers and his real boy's braces, with a real boy's haircut, smiling and smiling, and looking very pleased.

'No curls now,' said Bad Harry. 'Not any more.'

'No curls,' said my naughty little sister.

'No,' Bad Harry's mother said, 'and oh dear, you don't even *look* good any more.'

Then my sister laughed and laughed. 'Bad Harry!' she said. 'Bad Harry. All bad now – like me!'

My Naughty Little Sister can be a good girl sometimes!

*But my sister hadn't meant to be naughty.
She thought she had given the book-little-boy
her own supper, and you know she was quite
a greedy child, so it was a kind thing to do really.*

My Naughty Little Sister
and the book-little-boy

D o you like having stories read to you? When I was a little
girl I used to like it very much. My sister liked it too, but
she pretended that she didn't.

When my sister and I were very little children we had a kind
aunt who used to come and read stories to us. She used to read
all the stories that she'd had read to her when *she* was a little girl.

I used to listen and listen and say, 'Go on! Go on!' whenever my
auntie stopped for a minute, but my little sister used to pretend
that she wasn't listening. Wasn't she silly? She used to fidget with
her old doll, Rosy-Primrose, and pretend that she was playing
babies with her, but really she listened and listened too, and heard
every word.

Do you know how I knew that she listened and listened? I'll
tell you. When my little sister was in bed at night she used to tell
the stories all over again to Rosy-Primrose.

One day when my aunt came to read to us, she said, 'I've got a book here that I won as a Sunday School prize. I used to like these stories when I was a child, I hope you will like them too.'

So our aunt read us a story about a poor little boy. It was a very sad story in the beginning because this poor boy was very ragged and hungry. It said that he had no breakfast and no dinner and no supper, but it was lovely at the end because a nice kind lady took him home with her and said she was his real mother and gave him lots of nice things to eat and lots of nice clothes to wear, and a white pony. But the 'nothing to eat' part was very sad.

Now, do you know, my little sister liked eating, and she was so surprised to hear about the book-little-boy with nothing to eat that she forgot to pretend that she wasn't listening and she said, 'No breakfast?' She said 'no breakfast' in a very little voice.

Our auntie said, 'No, no breakfast.'

My little sister said, 'No dinner?' She said that in a little voice too, because she thought no dinner and no breakfast was terrible.

My aunt said, 'No dinner, *and* no supper,' and she was so pleased to think that my funny little sister *had* been listening that she said, 'Would you like to see the picture?' And my little sister said 'please' and I said 'please' too.

So our kind aunt showed us the picture in the book that went with the poor little boy story. It was a very miserable picture,

because the little boy was sitting all alone
in the corner of a room, looking very sad.
There was an empty plate on the floor
beside this poor little boy, and under
the picture it said, '*Nothing to eat.*'

Wasn't that sad?

My little sister thought it was very
sad. She looked and looked at the
picture and she said, 'No breakfast,
no dinner, and *no supper.*' Like that, over and over again.

My aunt said, 'Cheer up. He had lots to eat when his kind rich
mother took him home in the end; he had a pony too, remember,'
my aunt said.

But my sister said, 'No *picture* dinner. Poor, poor boy,' she said.

Well now, when the reading time was over my little sister was
a very quiet child. She was very quiet when she had her supper.
She sat by the fire and my mother gave her a big piece of buttery
bread and a big mug of warm sweet milk, but she was very quiet,
she said, 'thank you' in a tiny quiet voice, and she drank up her
milk like a good child. When my mother came to say that the
hot-water bottle was in her bed, she said her prayers at once and
went straight upstairs.

My mother kissed my warm little sister and said 'good night'. But when my kind aunt kissed her and said, 'good night' to her, my little sister said, '*No* breakfast, *no* dinner,' and my auntie said, 'No supper,' but my little sister smiled and said, '*Yes, supper.*' My little sister looked very smiley and pleased with herself.

When our aunt went to go home, and looked for the Sunday School prize-book, she knew why my little sister had said such a funny thing.

Do you know what that silly child had done? She had put her piece of buttery bread inside the Sunday School prize-book, on top of the little book boy's picture. She had given her supper to the book-little-boy!

Of course the book was very greasy and crumby after that, which was a pity because our aunt had kept it very tidy indeed as it had been a prize. I suppose it was a very naughty thing to have done.

But my little sister hadn't *meant* to be naughty. She thought that she had given the book-little-boy her own supper, and you know she was quite a greedy child, so it was a kind thing to do really.

Now you know why she said, '*No* breakfast, *no* dinner, and *yes, supper,*' don't you?

My Naughty Little Sister and the big girl's bed

A long time ago, when my naughty little sister was a very small girl, she had a nice cot with pull-up sides so that she couldn't fall out and bump herself.

My little sister's cot was a very pretty one. It was pink, and had pictures of fairies and bunny-rabbits painted on it.

It had been my old cot when I was a small child and I had taken care of the pretty pictures. I used to kiss the fairies 'good night' when I went to bed, but my bad little sister did not kiss them and take care of their pictures. Oh no!

My naughty little sister did dreadful things to those poor fairies. She scribbled on them with pencils and scratched them with tin-lids, and knocked them with poor old Rosy-Primrose her doll, until there were hardly any pictures left at all. She said, 'Nasty fairies. Silly old rabbits.'

There! Wasn't she a bad child? You wouldn't do things like that, would you?

And my little sister jumped and jumped on her cot. After she had been tucked up at night-time she would get out from under the covers, and jump and jump. And when she woke up in the morning she jumped and jumped again, until one day, when she was jumping, the bottom fell right out of the cot, and my naughty little sister, and the mattress, and the covers, and poor Rosy-Primrose all fell out on to the floor!

Then our mother said, 'That child must have a bed!' Even though our father managed to mend the cot, our mother said, 'She must have a bed!'

My naughty little sister said, 'A big bed for me?'

And our mother said, 'I am afraid so, you bad child. You are too rough now for your poor old cot.'

My little sister wasn't ashamed of being too rough for her cot. She was pleased because she was going to have a new bed, and she said, 'A big girl's bed for me!'

My little sister told everybody that she was going to have a big girl's bed. She told her kind friend the window-cleaner man, and the coalman, and the milkman. She told the dustman too. She said, 'You can have my old cot soon, dustman, because I am going to have a big girl's bed.' And she was as pleased as pleased.

But our mother wasn't pleased at all. She was rather worried. You see, our mother was afraid that my naughty little sister would jump and jump on her new bed, and scratch it, and treat it badly. My naughty little sister had done such dreadful things to her old cot, that my mother was afraid she would spoil the new bed too.

Well now, my little sister told the lady who lived next door all about her new bed. The lady who lived next door to us was called Mrs Jones, but my little sister used to call her Mrs Cocoa Jones because she used to go in and have a cup of cocoa with her every morning.

Mrs Cocoa Jones was a very kind lady, and when she heard about the new bed she said, 'I have a little yellow eiderdown and a yellow counterpane upstairs, and they are too small for any of my beds, so when your new bed comes, I will give them to you.'

My little sister was excited, but when she told our mother what Mrs Cocoa had said, our mother shook her head.

'Oh, dear,' she said, 'what will happen to the lovely eiderdown and counterpane when our bad little girl has them?'

Then, a kind aunt who lived near us said, 'I have a dear little green nightie-case put away in a drawer. It belonged to me when I was a little girl. When your new bed comes you can have it to put your nighties in like a big girl.'

My little sister said, 'Good. Good,' because of all the nice things she was going to have for her bed. But our mother was more worried than ever. She said, 'Oh dear! That pretty nightie-case. You'll spoil it, I know you will!'

But my little sister went on being pleased as pleased about it.

Then one day the new bed arrived. It was a lovely shiny brown bed, new as new, with a lovely blue stripy mattress to go on it: new as new. And there was a new stripy pillow too. Just like a real big girl would have.

My little sister watched while my mother took the poor old cot to pieces, and stood it up against the wall. She watched when the new bed was put up, and the new mattress was laid on top of it. She watched the new pillow being put into a clean white case, and when our mother made the bed with clean new sheets and clean new blankets, she said, 'Really, big-girl! A big girl's bed – all for me.'

Then Mrs Cocoa Jones came in, and she was carrying the pretty yellow eiderdown and the yellow counterpane. They were very

shiny and satiny like buttercup flowers, and when our mother put
them on top of the new bed, they looked beautiful.

Then our kind aunt came down the road, and she was carrying a
little parcel, and in the little parcel was the pretty green nightie-case.
My little sister ran down the road to meet her because she was so
excited. She was more excited still when our aunt picked up her
little nightdress and put it into the pretty green case and laid the
green case on the yellow shiny eiderdown.

My little sister was so pleased that she was glad when bedtime
came.

And, what do you think? She got carefully, carefully into bed with Rosy-Primrose, and she laid herself down and stretched herself out – carefully, carefully like a good, nice girl.

And she didn't jump and jump, and she didn't scratch the shiny brown wood, or scribble with pencils or scrape with tin-lids. Not ever! Not even when she had had the new bed a long, long time.

My little sister took great care of her big girl's bed. She took great care of her shiny yellow eiderdown and counterpane and her pretty green nightie-case.

And whatever do you think she said to me?

She said, 'You had the fairy pink cot before I did. But this is my very own big girl's bed, and I am going to take great care of my very own bed like a big girl!'

My Naughty Little Sister
does knitting

One day, when I was a little girl, and my naughty little sister was another little girl, a kind lady came to live next door to us. This kind lady's really true name was Mrs Jones, but my little sister always called her Mrs Cocoa Jones.

Do you know why she called her that? Shall I tell you? Well, it was because Mrs Cocoa Jones used to give my naughty little sister a cup of cocoa every morning.

Yes, every single morning, when it was eleven o'clock, Mrs Cocoa Jones used to bang hard on her kitchen wall with the handle of her floor-brush, and as our kitchen was right the other side of the wall, my naughty little sister could hear very well, and would bang and bang back to show that she was quite ready.

Then, my little sister would go into Mrs Cocoa Jones's house to drink cocoa with her. Wasn't that a nice idea?

My little sister used to go in to see Mrs Cocoa Jones so much that Mr Cocoa Jones make a little low gate between his garden and our father's garden so that my little sister could pop in without having to go all round the front of the houses each time. Mr Cocoa Jones made a nice little archway over the gate, and planted a little rose-tree to climb over it, especially for her. Wasn't she a fortunate child?

So you see, Mrs Cocoa Jones was a very great friend.

Well now, Mrs Cocoa Jones was a lady who was always knitting and knitting, and as she hadn't any little boys and girls of her own, she used to knit a lot of lovely woollies for my naughty little sister, and for me.

She knitted us red jumpers and blue jumpers, and yellow jumpers and red caps and blue caps and yellow caps to match, and she also knitted a blue jumper for Rosy-Primrose, who was my naughty little sister's favourite doll, and when she had finished all the caps and jumpers, she made us lots of pairs of socks. So, every time we saw Mrs Cocoa, she always had a bag of wool and a lot of clicky needles.

Sometimes, when Mrs Cocoa Jones wanted the wool wound up, she would ask my naughty little sister to hold it for her, and that fidgety child would drop it and tangle it, until Mr Cocoa Jones used to say, 'It looks to me as if you will be doing knotting not knitting with that lot,' to Mrs Cocoa. And my funny little sister would laugh and laugh because she thought it was very funny to say 'knotting' like that.

Now, one day Mrs Cocoa Jones said, 'Would you like to learn to knit?' to my naughty little sister.

'Would you like to learn to knit?' she asked my little sister, and my little sister said, 'Not very much.'

Then Mrs Cocoa Jones said, 'Well, but think of all the nice things you could make for everyone. You could knit Christmas presents and birthday presents all by yourself.'

Then my naughty little sister thought it would be rather nice to learn to knit, so she said, 'All right then, Mrs Cocoa Jones, would you please teach me?'

So Mrs Cocoa Jones lent her a pair of rather bendy needles and she gave her some wool, and she showed her how to knit. So, carefully, carefully my little sister learned to put the wool round the needle, and carefully, carefully to bring it out and make a stitch, and carefully, carefully to make another until she could really truly knit.

Then my naughty little sister was very pleased because she had a good idea. She thought that as Mr Cocoa Jones had made her such a nice little gate, she would knit him a scarf for his birthday, because his old scarf had got all moth-holey. The naughty little baby moths had eaten bits of his scarf and made holes in it, so my little sister thought he would like a new one very much.

She didn't tell anyone about it. Not even Mrs Cocoa Jones, she wanted it to be a real secret.

Well now, Mrs Cocoa had given my little sister all her odds and endsy bits of wool, and the red bits and the blue bits and the yellow bits from our jumpers, and some grey and purple and white and black and brown bits as well, so my little sister thought she would make a beautiful scarf.

She went secretly, secretly into corners to knit this beautiful scarf for Mr Cocoa Jones's birthday. Wasn't she a clever child?

She kept it carefully hidden all the time she wasn't making it. She hid it in a lot of funny places too. She hid it under her pillow, and in the coal-shed and behind the settee, and in the flour-tub. But most of the time she was knitting and knitting to have it made in time. So that, when Mr Cocoa Jones's birthday did come, it was quite ready and quite finished.

It was a very pretty scarf because of all the pretty colours my little sister had used, and although it was a bit coaly and a bit floury here and there, it still looked very lovely, and Mr Cocoa Jones was very pleased with it.

He said, 'It's the best scarf I have ever had!'

Then my little sister told him all about how she had knitted it, and she showed him some holes in it too, where the stitches had dropped, and Mr Cocoa Jones said they would make nice homes for the baby moths to live in anyway, so my little sister was glad she had dropped the stitches.

Then Mr Cocoa Jones said that as it was the very nicest scarf he had ever had knitted for him, it would be a shame to waste it by wearing it every day. So he said he would get Mrs Cocoa to put it away for him for High Days and Holidays.

So Mrs Cocoa wrapped it up very neatly and nicely in blue laundry paper, and she let my little sister put it away in Mr Cocoa's drawer for him, and Mr Cocoa wore his old scarf for every day until Mrs Cocoa had time to knit him another one.

The icy-cold tortoise

Long ago, when I was a little girl and had a little sister, we lived next door to a kind lady called Mrs Jones. My sister used to call this lady Mrs Cocoa sometimes.

If my mother had to go out and couldn't take my little sister this kind next-door lady used to mind her. My sister was always glad to be minded by dear Mrs Jones and Mrs Cocoa Jones was always glad to mind my little sister. They enjoyed minding days very much.

Well now, one cold blowy day when the wind was pulling all the old leaves off the trees to make room for the new baby ones to grow, our mother asked Mrs Cocoa Jones to mind my sister while she went shopping.

Mrs Cocoa and my sister had a lovely time. They swept up all the leaves from Mr Jones's nice tidy paths and put them into a heap for him to burn. They went indoors and laid Mr Jones's tea, and they were just going to sit down by the fire to have a rest when they heard Mr Cocoa coming down the back path.

Mr Cocoa came down the path pushing his bicycle with one hand

and holding a very strange-looking wooden box with holes in it
in the other hand.

When Mr Jones saw my little sister peeping at him out of his
kitchen window he smiled and smiled. 'Hello, Mrs Pickle,' he said.
'What are you doing here, then?'

'I'm being minded,' said my little sister. Then, because she
was an inquisitive child she said, 'What have you got in that box,
Mr Cocoa?'

'Just wait a minute,
and I'll show you,'
Mr Cocoa said, and he
went off to put his
bicycle in the shed.

'I wonder what's in
that box, Mrs Cocoa?'
said my inquisitive
little sister.

'It's a very funny
box – it's got holes in it.'

'Ah,' said Mrs Cocoa,
'just you wait and see!'

When kind Mr Cocoa came in and saw my impatient little sister he was so good he didn't even stop to take off his coat. He opened the box at once – and he showed my sister an icy-cold tortoise, lying fast asleep under a lot of hay.

Have you ever seen a tortoise? My little sister hadn't.

Tortoises are very strange animals. They have hard round shells and long crinkly necks and little beaky noses. They have tiny black eyes and four scratchy-looking claws.

But when they are asleep you can't see their heads or their claws; they are tucked away under their shells. They just look like cold round stones.

My little sister thought the tortoise was a stone at first. She touched it, and it was icy-cold. 'What is it?' she said. 'What is this stone-thing?'

Mr Cocoa picked the tortoise up and showed her where the little claws were tucked away, and the beaky little shut-eyed face under the shell.

'It's a tortoise,' Mr Cocoa said.

'He's having his winter sleep now,' said Mrs Cocoa.

Mr Jones told my sister that one of the men who worked with him had given him the tortoise, because he was going away and wouldn't have anywhere to keep it in his new home.

'I shall put him away in the cupboard under the stairs now,' he
said. 'He will sleep there all the winter and wake up again when
the warm days come.'

Just as Mr Cocoa said this, the tortoise opened its little beady
black eyes and looked at my sister. Then it closed them and went to
sleep again. So Mr Cocoa put it away in its box right at the back of
the cupboard under the stairs.

'That's a funny animal,' my naughty little sister said.

After that, she talked and talked about the tortoise. She kept
saying, 'When will it wake up – When *will* it wake up?' But it didn't
so she got tired of asking. By the time Christmas came she had
almost forgotten it. And when the snow fell she quite forgot it.

And when spring came and the birds began to sing again, and
she went in one day to have her morning cocoa with her next-door
friend, Mrs Jones had forgotten it too!

They were just drinking their cocoa and Mrs Jones was telling
my naughty little sister about some of the things she had done
when she was a little girl when they heard:

Thump! Thump! Bang! Bang!

'Oh dear,' said Mrs Cocoa. 'There's someone at the front door!'
And she went to look. But there wasn't.

Thump! Thump!

'It must be the back door,' said Mrs Cocoa Jones, and she went to look but it wasn't!

Bang! Bang!

'What can it be?' asked Mrs Jones.

Now, my clever little sister had been listening hard. 'It's in the under-the-stairs place, Mrs Cocoa,' she said. 'Listen.'

Thump! Thump! Bang! Bang!

'Oh goodness,' said Mrs Cocoa. But she was a very brave lady. She opened the door of the cupboard and looked and my little sister looked too.

And Mrs Cocoa stared and my little sister stared.

There was the tortoise's wooden box, shaking and bumping because the cross tortoise inside had woken up and was banging to be let out.

'Goodness me,' said Mrs Cocoa. 'That tortoise has woken up!'

'Goodness me,' said my funny little sister. 'That tortoise has woken up!'

And Mrs Cocoa looked hard at my sister and my sister looked hard at her.

'I shall have to see to it,' Mrs Cocoa said, and she picked up the bumping box and carried it into her kitchen and put the box on the table. Then she lifted my sister up to the chair so she could watch.

Mrs Cocoa lifted the lid off the box, and there was that wide-awake tortoise. His head was waggle-waggling and his claws scratch-scratching to get out.

'I used to have a tortoise when I was a girl,' Mrs Cocoa said, 'so I know just what to do!'

And do you know what she did? She put some warm water into a bowl, and she put the tortoise in the warm water. Then she took it out and dried it very, very carefully on an old soft towel.

Then Mrs Cocoa put the clean fresh tortoise on the table, and said, 'Just mind it while I go and get it something to eat, there's a good child. Just put your hand gently on his back and he will stay quite still.'

My little sister did keep her hand on the tortoise's back and he was quite still until Mrs Cocoa came back with a cabbage leaf.

'Look,' my naughty little sister said, 'look at his waggly head, Mrs Jones.'

And she put her face right down so she could see his little black eyes. 'Hello, Mr Tortoise,' she said.

And the tortoise made a funny noise at her. It said, 'His-ss-SS.'

My poor sister was surprised! She didn't like that noise very much. But Mrs Cocoa said the tortoise had only said, 'His-ss-SS' because it was hungry and not because it was cross. Mrs Cocoa said tortoises are nice friendly things so long as you let them go their own way.

And because my sister had minded the tortoise for her she let her give him the cabbage leaf.

At first he only looked at it, and pushed it about with his beaky head, but at last he bit a big piece out of it.

'There!' Mrs Jones said. 'That's the first thing he's tasted since last summer!'

Just fancy that!

Mr Cocoa made the tortoise a little home in his rockery where it could sleep, and it could walk around among the stones or hide among the rockery flowers if it wanted to.

Sometimes it used to eat the flowers, and make Mr Cocoa cross.

That tortoise lived with the Cocoa Joneses for many, many years. It slept under the stairs in the winter and walked about the rockery in summer. It was still there when my sister was a grown-up lady.

Mr and Mrs Cocoa called it Henry, but of course when my sister was little she always called it Henry Cocoa Jones.

My Naughty Little Sister
makes a bottle-tree

One day, when I was a little girl, and my naughty little sister was a little girl, my naughty little sister got up very early one morning, and while my mother was cooking the breakfast, my naughty little sister went quietly, quietly out of the kitchen door, and quietly, quietly up the garden-path. Do you know why she went *quietly* like that? It was because she was *up to mischief.*

She didn't stop to look at the flowers, or the marrows or the runner-beans and she didn't put her fingers in the water-tub. No! She went right along to the tool-shed to find a trowel. You know what trowels are, of course, but my naughty little sister didn't. She called the trowel a 'digger'.

'Where is the digger?' said my naughty little sister to herself.

Well, she found the trowel, and she took it down the garden until she came to a very nice place in the big flower-bed. Then she stopped and began to dig and dig with the trowel, which you know was a most naughty thing to do, because of all the little baby seeds

that are waiting to come up in flower-beds sometimes.

Shall I tell you why my naughty little sister dug that hole? All right. I will. It was because she wanted to plant a brown shiny acorn. So, when she had made a really nice deep hole, she put the acorn in it, and covered it all up again with earth, until the brown shiny acorn was all gone.

Then my naughty little sister got a stone, and a leaf, and a stick, and she put them on top of the hole, so that she could remember where the acorn was, and then she went indoors to have her hands washed for breakfast. She didn't tell me, or my mother or anyone about the acorn. She kept it for her secret.

Well now, my naughty little sister kept going down the garden all that day, to look at the stone, the leaf and the stick, on top of her acorn-hole, and my naughty little sister smiled and smiled to herself because she knew that there was a brown shiny acorn under the earth.

But when my father came home, he was very cross. He said, 'Who's been digging in my flowerbed?'

And my little sister said, 'I have.'

Then my father said, 'You are a bad child. You've disturbed all the little baby seeds!'

And my naughty little sister said, 'I don't care about the little baby seeds, I want a home for my brown shiny acorn.'

So my father said, 'Well, *I* care about the little baby seeds, so I shall dig your acorn up for you, and you must find another home for it,' and he dug it up for her at once, and my naughty little sister tried all over the garden to find a new place for her acorn.

But there were beans and marrows and potatoes and lettuce and tomatoes and roses and spinach and radishes, and no room at all for the acorn, so my naughty little sister grew crosser and crosser and when tea-time came she wouldn't eat her tea. Aren't you glad you don't show off like that?

Then my mother said, 'Now don't be miserable. Eat up your tea and you shall help me to plant your acorn in a bottleful of water.'

So my naughty little sister ate her tea after all, and then my mother, who was a clever woman, filled a bottle with water, and showed my naughty little sister how to put the acorn in the top of the bottle. Shall I tell you how she did it, in case you want to try?

Well now, my naughty little sister put the pointy end of the acorn into the water, and left the bottom of the acorn sticking out of the top (the bottom end, you know, is the end that sits in the little cup when it's on the tree).

'Now,' said my mother, 'you can watch its little root grow in the water.'

My naughty little sister had to put her acorn in lots of bottles of water, because the bottles were always getting broken, as she put them in such funny places. She put them on the kitchen window-sill where the cat walked, and on the side of the bath, and inside the bookcase, until my mother said, 'We'll put it on top of the cupboard, and I will get it down for you to see every morning after breakfast.'

Then at last, the little root began to grow. It pushed down, down into the bottle of water and it made lots of other little roots that looked just like whitey fingers, and my naughty little sister was

pleased as pleased. Then, one day, a little shoot came out of the top of the acorn, and broke all the browny outside off, and on this little shoot were two tiny baby leaves, and the baby leaves grew and grew, and my mother said, 'That little shoot will be a big tree one day.'

My naughty little sister was very pleased. When she was pleased she danced and danced, so you can just guess how she danced to think of her acorn growing into a tree.

'Oh,' she said, 'when it's a tree we can put a swing on it, and I can swing indoors on my very own tree.'

But my mother said, 'Oh, no. I'm afraid it won't like being indoors very much now, it will want to grow out under the sky.'

Then my naughty little sister had a good idea. And now, this is a *good thing* about my little sister – she had a *very kind thought* about her little tree. She said, 'I know! When we go for a walk we'll take my bottle-tree and the digger' (which, of course, you call a trowel) 'and we will plant it in the park, just where there are no trees, so it can grow and grow and spread and spread into a big tree.'

And that is just what she did do. Carefully, carefully, she took her bottle-tree out of the bottle, and put it in her basket, and then we all went out to the park. And when my little sister had found a good place for her little bottle-tree, she dug a nice deep hole for it, and then she put her tree into the hole, and gently, gently put the earth all round its roots, until only the leaves and the stem were showing, and when she'd planted it in, my mother showed her how to pat the earth with the trowel.

Then at last the little tree was in the kind of place it really liked, and my little sister had planted it all by herself.

Now you will be pleased to hear that the little bottle-tree grew and grew and now it's quite a big tree. Taller than my naughty little sister, and she's quite a big lady nowadays.

Very Naughty stories indeed!

*She started to yell and stamp, and make such
a noise that people going by looked over
the hedge to see what the matter was.*

Going fishing

One day, when I was a little girl, and my sister was a very little girl, some children came to our house and asked my mother if I could go fishing with them.

They had jam-jars with string on them, and fishing-nets and sandwiches and lemonade.

My mother said, 'Yes' – I could go with them; and she found me a jam-jar and a fishing-net, and cut *me* some sandwiches.

Then my naughty little sister said, 'I want to go! I want to go!' Just like that. So my mother said I might as well take her too.

Then my mother cut some sandwiches for my little sister, but she didn't give her a jam-jar or a fishing-net because she said she was too little to go near the water. My mother gave my little sister a basket to put stones in, because my little sister liked to pick up stones, and she gave me a big bottle of lemonade to carry for both of us.

My mother said, 'You mustn't let your little sister get herself wet. You must keep her away from the water.' And I said, 'All right, Mother, I promise.'

So then we went off to the little river, and we took our shoes
off and our socks off and tucked up our clothes, and we went
into the water to catch fish with our fishing-nets, and we filled
our jam-jars with water to put the fishes in when we caught them.
And we said to my naughty little sister, 'You mustn't come, you'll get
yourself wet.'

Well, we paddled and paddled and fished and fished, but we didn't catch any fish at all, not one little tiny one even. Then a boy said, 'Look, there is your little sister in the water too!'

And, do you know, my naughty little sister had walked right into the water with her shoes and socks on, and she was trying to fish with her little basket.

I said, 'Get out of the water,' and she said, 'No.'

I said, 'Get out at *once*,' and she said, 'I don't want to.'

I said, 'You'll get all wet,' and she said, 'I don't care.' Wasn't she naughty?

So I said, 'I must fetch you out then,' and my naughty little sister tried to run away in the water. Which is a silly thing to do because she fell down and got all wet.

She got her frock wet, and her petticoat wet, and her knickers wet, and her vest wet, and her hair wet, and her hair-ribbon – all soaking wet. Of course, I told you her shoes and socks were wet before.

And she cried and cried.

So we fetched her out of the water, and we said, 'Oh, dear, she will catch a cold,' and we took off her wet frock, and her wet petticoat and her wet knickers and her wet vest, and her wet hair-ribbon, *and* her wet shoes and socks, and we hung all the things to

dry on the bushes in the sunshine,
and we wrapped my naughty little
sister in a woolly cardigan.

My little sister *cried and cried.*

So we gave her the sandwiches,
and she ate them all up. She ate up
her sandwiches and my sandwiches,
and the other children's sandwiches
all up – and she cried and cried.

Then we gave her the
lemonade and she spilled it
all over the grass, and she cried and cried.

Then one of the children gave her an apple, and another of
the children gave her some toffees, and while she was eating these,
we took her clothes off the bushes and ran about with them in the
sunshine until they were dry. When her clothes were quite dry, we
put them all back on her again, and she screamed and screamed
because she didn't want her clothes on any more.

So, I took her home, and my mother said, 'Oh, you've let your
little sister fall into the water.'

And I said, 'How do you know? Because we dried all her clothes,'
and my mother said, 'Ah, but you didn't *iron* them.' My little

sister's clothes were all crumpled and messy.

Then my mother said that I should not have any sugary biscuits for supper because I was disobedient. Only bread and butter, and she said my little sister must go straight to bed, and have some hot milk to drink.

And my mother said to my little sister, 'Don't you think you were a naughty little girl to go into the water?'

And my naughty little sister said, 'I won't do it any more, because it was too wet.'

But, do you know, when my mother went to throw away the stones out of my little sister's basket, she found a little fish in the bottom which my naughty little sister had caught!

Crusts

A long time ago, when my sister was a little girl, she didn't like eating bread-and-butter crusts.

Our mother was very cross about this, because she had to eat crusts when *she* was a little girl, and she thought my sister should eat her crusts up too!

Every day at tea-time, Mother would put a piece of bread-and-butter on our plates and say, '*Plain* first. *Jam* second, and *cake if you're lucky!*'

She would say, '*Plain* first. *Jam* second, and *cake if you're lucky,*' because that is what our granny used to say to her when she was a little girl.

That meant that we ought to eat plain bread-and-butter before we had some with jam on, and all the bread – even the crusts – or we wouldn't get any cake.

I always ate *my* piece of bread-and-butter up straight away like a good girl, but my naughty little sister didn't. She used to bend her piece in half and nibble out the middle soft part and leave the crust on her plate.

Sometimes she played games with the crust – she would hold it up and peep through the hole and say, 'I see you.'

Sometimes she would put her hand through it and say, 'I've got a wristwatch!' And sometimes she would break it up into little pieces and leave them all over the table cloth. But she never, never ate it. Wasn't she a wasteful child?

Then, when she'd stopped playing with her bread-and-butter crust my bad little sister would say, 'Cake.'

'Cake,' she would say, 'Cake – *please.*'

Our mother would say, 'What about that crust? Aren't you going to eat it?'

And my naughty little sister would shake her head. 'All messy. Nasty crust,' she would say.

'No crust. No cake,' Mother said. But it didn't make any difference though. My bad sister said, 'I'll get down then!'

And if anyone tried to make her eat her crust she would scream and scream.

Our mother didn't know what to do. She told Mrs next-door Cocoa Jones and Mrs Cocoa said, 'Try putting something nice on the crusts. See if she will eat them then!'

Mrs Cocoa said, 'She loves pink fish-paste, try that.'

So next day at tea-time our mother said, 'Will you eat your crusts up if I put pink fish-paste on them?'

And my naughty little sister said, 'Oh, pink fish-paste!' because that was a very great treat. 'I like pink fish-paste,' my sister said.

So our mother put some pink fish-paste on the crust that my little sister had left.

'Now eat it up,' Mother said.

But my sister didn't eat her crust after all. No. Do you know what she did? She licked all the fish-paste off her crust and then she put it back on her plate and said, 'Finished. No cake. Get down now.'

Wasn't she a naughty girl?

One day during the time when my sister wouldn't eat crusts Bad Harry and his mother came to tea at our house.

When Bad Harry's mother saw that my little sister wasn't eating her crusts she was very surprised. She said, 'Why aren't you eating your crusts?'

My sister said, 'I don't like them.'

Bad Harry's mother said, 'But you always eat your crusts when you come to our house. You eat them all up then, just like Harry does.'

We were amazed when we heard Bad Harry's mother say that. She said, 'They don't leave crust or crumb!' But my naughty little sister didn't say anything and Bad Harry didn't say anything either.

When our father came home from work and Mother told him about my sister eating her crusts at Harry's house, Father was very stern.

'That shows you've got to be firm with that child,' he said, and he shook his finger at my sister.

'No more crusts left on plates. I *mean* it.' He did look cross.

And my naughty little sister said in a tiny little voice. 'No crusts like Harry? No crusts like Bad Harry.'

And Father said, 'No crusts like *Good* Harry. No crusts or *I will know the reason why.*'

So after that there were no more crusts on my little sister's plate and she ate cake after that like everyone else.

But one day, a long time afterwards when our mother was spring-cleaning, she was dusting under the table, and saw some funny green mossy-stuff growing out from a crack underneath the table-top.

This crack belonged to a little drawer that had lost its handle and hadn't been opened for a long time.

Mother said, 'Goodness. What on earth is that?' And she went and fetched something to hook into the drawer, and then she tried to pull it out. It took a long time because the drawer was stuck.

Mother pulled and prodded and tapped and all of a sudden the drawer rushed out so quickly it fell on to the floor.

And all over the floor was a pile of green mouldy crusts!

My naughty little sister had found that crack under the table and

pushed all her crusts into the drawer when no one was looking!

My sister was very surprised to see all that mossy-looking old bread. She had forgotten all about it.

When Mother scolded her she said, 'I must have been very naughty. I eat my crusts now though, don't I?'

'And we thought you were being good like Harry,' our mother said, and then my sister laughed and laughed.

And do you want to know why she did that? Well, a long time after that, Harry's father got the gas-men to put a new stove in their kitchen, and when the gas-men took the old gas-cooker out they found lots and lots of old dried-up crusts behind it.

When our mother heard about this, she laughed too. 'Fancy us expecting you to learn anything good from that Bad Harry,' she said.

My Naughty Little Sister cuts out

O nce, when I was a little girl, and my naughty little sister was a very little girl, it rained and rained and rained. It rained every day, and it rained all the time, and everything got wetter and wetter and wetter, and when my naughty little sister went out she had to wear her mackintosh and her wellingtons.

My naughty little sister had a beautiful red mackintosh-cape with a hood – just like Little Red Riding Hood's – and she had a little red umbrella.

My little sister used to carry her umbrella under her cape, because she didn't want it to get wet. Wasn't she a silly girl?

When my naughty little sister went down the road, the rain went *plop, plop, plop, plop*, on to her head, and *scatter-scatter-scatter* against her

cape, and her wellington boots went *splish-splosh, splish-splosh* in the puddles.

My naughty little sister liked puddles very much, and she splished and sploshed such a lot that the water got into the tops of her wellingtons and made her feet wet inside, and then my naughty little sister was very sorry, because she caught a cold.

She got a nasty, sneezy, atishoo-y cold, and couldn't go out in the rain any more. My poor little sister looked very miserable when my mother said she could not go out. But her cold was very bad, and she had a red nose, and red eyes, and a nasty buzzy ear – all because of getting her feet wet, and every now and again – she couldn't help it – she said, 'A-a-tishoo!'

Now, my naughty little sister was a fidgety child. She wouldn't sit down quietly to hear a story like you do, or play nicely with a toy, or draw pictures with a pencil – she just fidgeted and wriggled and grumbled all the time, and said, 'Want to go out in the rain – want to splash and splash,' in the crossest and growliest voice, and then she said, 'A-a-tishoo!' even when she didn't want to, because of the nasty cold she'd got. And she grumbled and grumbled and grumbled.

My mother made her an orange drink, but she grumbled. My mother gave her cough stuff, but she grumbled, and really no one knew how to make her good. My mother said, 'Why don't you look at a picture-book?' And my naughty little sister said, 'No book, nasty book.'

Then my mother said, 'Well, would you like to play with my button-box?' and my naughty little sister said she thought she might like that. But when she had dropped all the buttons out and spilled them all over the floor, she said, 'No buttons, tired of buttons. A-a-tishoo!' She said, 'A-a-tishoo' like that, because she couldn't help it.

My mother said, 'Dear me, what can I do for the child?'

Then my mother had a good idea. She said, 'I know, you can make a scrap-book!'

So my mother found a big book with clean pages and a lot of old birthday cards and Christmas cards, and some old picture-books, and a big pot of sticky paste, and she showed my naughty little sister how to make a scrap-book.

My naughty little sister was quite pleased, because she had never

115

been allowed to use scissors before, and these were the nice snippy ones from Mother's work-box.

My naughty little sister cut out a picture of a cow, and a basket with roses in, and a lady in a red dress, and a house and a squirrel, and she stuck them all in the big book with the sticky paste, and then she laughed and laughed.

Do you know why she laughed? She laughed because she had stuck them all in the book in a funny way. She stuck the lady in first, and then she put the basket of roses on the lady's head, and the cow on top of that, and then she put the house and the squirrel under the lady's feet. My naughty little sister thought that the lady looked very funny with the basket of flowers and the cow on her head.

So my naughty little sister amused herself for quite a long while, and my mother said, 'Thank goodness,' and went upstairs to tidy the bedrooms, as my naughty little sister wasn't grumbling any more.

But that naughty child soon got tired of the scrap-book, and when she got tired of it, she started rubbing all the sticky paste over the table and made the table all gummy. Wasn't that nasty of her?

Then she poked the scissors into the birthday cards and the Christmas cards, and made them look very ugly, and then, because she liked to do snip-snipping with the scissors, she looked around for something big to cut.

Fancy looking round for mischief like that! But she did. She didn't care at all, she just looked round for something to cut.

She snipped up all father's newspaper with the scissors, and she tried to snip the pussy-cat's tail, only pussy put her back up and said 'Pss', and frightened my naughty little sister.

So my naughty little sister looked round for something that she could cut up easily, and she found a big brown-paper parcel on a chair – a parcel all tied up with white string.

My naughty little sister was so bad because she couldn't go out to play in the wet, that she cut the string of the parcel. She knew that she shouldn't but she didn't care a bit. She cut the string right through, and pulled it all off. She did that because she thought it would be nice to cut up all the brown paper that was round the parcel.

So she dragged the parcel on to the floor, and began to pull off the brown paper. But when the brown paper was off, my very naughty little sister found something inside that she thought would be much nicer to cut. It was a lovely piece of silky, rustly material with little flowers all over it – the sort of special stuff that party-dresses are made of.

Now, my naughty little sister knew that she mustn't cut stuff like that but she didn't care. She thought she would just make a quick snip to see how it sounded when it was cut. So she did make a snip, and the stuff went *scc-scrr-scrr* as the scissors bit it, and my naughty little sister was so pleased that she forgot about everything else, and just cut and cut.

And then, all of a sudden . . . yes! *In came my mother!*

My mother was cross when she saw the sticky table, and the cut-up newspaper, but when she looked on the floor and saw my naughty little sister cutting the silky stuff, she was very, very angry.

'You are a bad, bad child,' my mother said. 'You shall not have the scissors any more. Your kind Aunt Betty is going to be married soon, and she sent this nice stuff for me to make you a bridesmaid's dress, because she wanted you to hold her dress in church for her. Now you won't be able to go.'

My naughty little sister cried and cried because she wanted to be a bridesmaid and because she liked to have new dresses very much. But it was no use, because the stuff was all cut up.

After that my naughty little sister tried to be a good girl until her cold was better.

When my father minded
My Naughty Little Sister

When my sister was a naughty little girl, she had a very cross friend. My little sister's cross friend was called Mr Blakey, and he was a very grumbly old man.

My little sister's friend Mr Blakey was the shoe-mender man, and he had a funny little shop with bits of leather all over the floor, and boxes of nails, and boot-polish, and shoe-laces, all over the place. Mr Blakey had a picture in his shop too. It was a very beautiful picture of a dog with boots on all four feet, walking in the rain. My little sister loved that picture very much, but she loved Mr Blakey better than that.

Every time we went in Mr Blakey's shop with our mother, my naughty little sister would start meddling with things, and Mr Blakey would say, 'Leave that be, you varmint,' in a very loud cross voice, and my little sister would stop meddling at once, just like an obedient child, because Mr Blakey was her favourite man, and one day, when we went into his shop, do you know what she did? She went straight behind the counter and kissed him *without being asked.* Mr Blakey was very surprised because he had a lot of nails in his mouth, but after that, he always gave her a peppermint humbug after he had shouted at her.

Well, that's about Mr Blakey in case you wonder who he was later on, now this is the real story:

One day, my mother had to go out shopping, so she asked my father if he would mind my naughty little sister for the day. My mother said she would take me shopping because I was a big girl, but my little sister was too draggy and moany to go to the big shops.

My father said he would mind my little sister, but my little sister said, 'I want to go, I want to go.' You know how she said that by now, I think. 'I want to go' – like that. And she kicked and screamed.

My mother said, 'Oh dear, how tiresome you are,' to my little sister, but my father said, 'You'll jolly well do as you're told, old lady.'

Then my naughty little sister wouldn't eat her breakfast, but my mother went off shopping with me just the same, and when we had gone, my father looked very fierce, and he said, 'What about that breakfast?'

So my naughty little sister ate all her breakfast up, every bit, and she said, 'More milk, please,' and 'More bread, please,' so much that my father got tired getting it for her.

Then, as it was a hot day, my father said, 'I'll bring my work into the garden, and give an eye to you at the same time.'

So my father took a chair and a table out into the garden, and my little sister went out into the garden too, and because my father was there she played good child's games. She didn't tread on the baby seedlings, or pick the flowers, or steal the black currants, or do anything at all wicked. She didn't want my father to look fierce again, and my father said she was a good nice child.

My little sister just sat on the lawn and played with Rosy-Primrose, and she made a tea-party with leaves and nasturtium seeds, and when she wanted something she asked my father for it nicely, not going off and finding it for herself at all.

She said, 'Please, Father, would you get me Rosy-Primrose's box?' and my father put down his pen, and his writing-paper, and got out of his chair, and went and got Rosy-Primrose's box, which was on the top shelf of the toy-cupboard and had all Rosy-Primrose's tatty old clothes in it.

Then my father did writing again, and then my little sister said, 'Please can I have a drink of water?' She said it nicely, 'Please,' she said.

That was very good of her to ask, but Father wasn't pleased at all, he said, 'Bother!' because he was being a busy man, and he

stamped and stamped to the kitchen to get the water for my polite little sister.

But my father didn't know about Rosy-Primrose's water. You see, when my little sister had a drink she always gave Rosy-Primrose a drink too in a blue doll's cup. So when my father brought back the water, my little sister said, 'Where is Rosy-Primrose's water?' and my cross father said, 'Bother Rosy-Primrose,' like that, cross and grumbly.

And my father was crosser and grumblier when my little sister asked him to put Rosy-Primrose's box back in the toy-cupboard, he said, 'That wretched doll again?' and he took Rosy-Primrose and shut her in the box too, and put it on top of the bookcase, to show how firm he was going to be. So then my little sister stopped being good.

She started to yell and stamp, and make such a noise that people going by looked over the hedge to see what the matter was. Wouldn't you have been ashamed if it were you stamping and yelling with people looking at you? My naughty little sister wasn't ashamed. She didn't care about the people at all, she was a stubborn bad child.

My father was a stubborn man too. He took his table and his chair and his writing things indoors and shut himself away in his study. 'You'll jolly well stay there till you behave,' he said to my naughty little sister.

My naughty little sister cried and cried until my father looked out of the window and said, 'Any more of that, and off to bed you go.' Then she was quiet, because she didn't want to go to bed.

She only peeped in once after that, but my father said, 'Go away, do,' and went on writing and writing, and he was so interested in his writing, he forgot all about my little sister, and it wasn't until he began to get hungry that he remembered her at all.

Then my father went out into the kitchen, and there was a lot of nice salad-stuff in the kitchen that our mother had left for lunch. There was junket too, and stewed pears, and biscuits for my father's and my little sister's lunches. My father remembered my little sister then, and he went to call her for lunch, because it was quite late. It was so late it was *four o'clock*.

But my little sister wasn't in the garden. My father looked and looked. He looked among the marrows, and behind the runner-bean

rows, and under the hedge. He looked in the shed and down the cellar-hole, but there was no little girl.

Then my father went indoors again and looked all over the house, and all the time he was calling and calling, but there was still no little girl at all.

Then my father was worried. He didn't stop to change his slippers or eat his lunch. He went straight out of the gate, and down the road to look for my little sister. But he couldn't see her at all. He asked people, 'Have you seen a little girl with red hair?' and people said, 'No.'

My father was just coming up the road again, looking so hot and so worried, when my mother and I got off the bus. When my mother saw him, she said, 'He's lost that child,' because she knows my father and my sister rather well.

When we got indoors my mother said, 'Why haven't you eaten your lunch?' and then my father told her all about the writing, and my bad sister. So my mother said, 'Well, if she's anywhere, she's near food of some kind, have you looked in the larder?' My father said he had. So Mother said, 'Well, I don't know –'

Then I said something clever, I said, 'I expect she is with old Mr Blakey.' So we went off to Mr Blakey's shop, and there she was. Fast asleep on a pile of leather bits.

Mr Blakey seemed quite cross with us for having lost her, and my naughty little sister was very cross when we took her away because she said she had had a lovely time with Mr Blakey. Mr Blakey had boiled her an egg in his tea-kettle, and given her some bread and cheese out of newspaper, and let her cut it for herself with one of his nice leathery knives. Mother was cross because she had been looking forward to a nice cup of tea after the bus journey, and I was cross because my little sister had had such a fine time in Mr Blakey's shop.

The only happy one was my father. He said, 'Thank goodness I can work again without having to concentrate on a disagreeable baby.' However, that made my sister cry again, so he wasn't happy for long.

My Naughty Little Sister
is very sorry

A long time ago, when I was a little girl with a naughty little sister, a cross lady lived in our road. This cross lady was called Mrs Lock and she didn't like children.

Mrs Lock didn't like children at all, and if she saw a boy or girl stopping by her front gate she would tap on her window to them and say, 'Don't hang about here,' in a very grumbling voice.

Wasn't that a cross thing to do? I will tell you why Mrs Lock was so cross. It was because she had a very beautiful garden outside her front door and once some boys had been playing football in the roadway, and the ball had bounced into her garden and broken down a beautiful rose-tree.

So when Mrs Lock saw children by her gate she thought they were going to start playing with footballs and damage her garden, and she always sent them away. Sometimes she came right out of the house and down to the gate and said, 'Go and play in the park – the roadway is no place for games,' and she would look so fierce and cross that the children would hurry away at once.

There was another reason too, why Mrs Lock was so cross. You see, she had a beautiful smoky-looking cat, and one day a nasty child had thrown a stone at the cat and hurt his poor leg, so if Mrs Lock saw a boy or girl stroking her smoky-looking cat, she would say, 'Don't you meddle with that cat, now!'

What a cross lady she was! But I suppose you couldn't really blame her. It isn't nice to have your rose-trees broken, and it's very, very bad to have your poor cat injured, isn't it?

Well now: one bright sunshiny morning, my naughty little sister went out for a little walk down the road all by herself. It was only a very small walk, just as far as the lamp-post at the corner of the road and back again, but my little sister was pretending that it was a very long walk; she was pretending that she was a shopping lady, stopping at all the hedges and gate-ways and saying that they were shops.

My little sister had a lovely game, all by herself, being a shopping-lady. It was a very nice day, and she had a little cane shopping-basket just like our mother's and a little old purse full of beads for pennies.

First my little sister stopped at a hedge and said, 'I'll have a nice cabbage today, please.' Then she picked a leaf and pretended that it was a cabbage, and put it carefully into her basket. She took two beads out of her purse and left them under the hedge to pay for it.

She went on until she came to a wall; there were two little round

stones by the wall, so she pretended that they were eggs and bought them too.

Then she found a piece of red flower-pot which made nice meat for her pretend dinner. She had a lovely game.

Just as she arrived at Mrs Lock's gate, the big smoky-looking cat jumped up on to it and began to purr and purr and as he purred his big feathery tail went all curly and twisty and he looked very beautiful. My sister stopped to look at him.

When the big smoky-looking cat saw my sister looking at him, he opened his mouth and showed her all his sharp little teeth, then he stretched out his curly pink tongue and began to lick one of his legs. He licked and licked.

My little sister was very pleased to see such a nice cat and she stood tippy-toed and touched him. When she did this he stopped licking and began to purr again.

He was nice and warm and furry, so she stroked him, very gently towards his tail because Mother had told us that pussies didn't like being stroked the other way. 'Dear Pussy. Nice animal,' she said to him.

Now, as my sister was such a little girl Mrs Lock didn't see her standing by the gate, so she didn't say 'go away' to her, and my sister had a long talk with the smoky-looking cat.

She told him that she
was a shopping-lady. 'I
have bought lots of things,'
she said. 'I can't think of
anything else.'

When she said this, the cat
got up suddenly and jumped right
off the gate back into Mrs Lock's
garden, and as he jumped the
gate opened wide. 'Meeow,' he
said. 'Meeow' – like that.

My bad little sister looked through the gate and she saw the smoky
cat going up the path. She saw all the pretty tulip flowers and the
wallflowers growing on each side, and do you know what she said?

She said, 'That was very kind of you, Pussy. Now I can buy a nice
cup to drink my milk out of.'

And she walked into Mrs Lock's garden. Mrs Lock's tulip flowers
were all different colours: red, yellow, pink and white. You know
that tulip flowers look rather like cups, don't you?

Yes. You know.

'I'll have a yellow cup, please,' my bad sister said. 'Here's the
money, Pussy.'

And she picked a yellow tulip head and put it in her basket.

The smoky-looking cat walked round and round her legs, and his long tickly tail waved and waved and he said, 'Purr' to my little sister who was pretending to be a shopping-lady.

And Mrs Lock saw her from her front window.

Mrs Lock *was* cross. She tapped hard on her window glass and my naughty little sister saw her. Then she remembered that she wasn't really a shopping-lady, she remembered that she was a little girl. She remembered that it was naughty to pick flowers that didn't belong to you.

Of course you know what she did? Yes. She ran away, through the gate and down the road to our house, while Mrs Lock tapped

and tapped and the smoky cat stood still in surprise.

My little sister ran straight indoors and straight upstairs and hid herself under the bed.

Mrs Lock came down the road after her, and when she saw my little sister run into the house, she came and knocked at our door, and told our mother all about my little sister's bad behaviour.

My mother was very sorry to hear that my sister had picked one of Mrs Lock's tulips, and when Mrs Lock had gone, our mother went upstairs and peeped under the bed. You see, she knew *just* where her naughty little girl would be.

'Come out,' Mother said in a kind voice, because she knew my little sister was ashamed of herself, and my little sister came out very

slowly, and stood by the side of the bed and looked very sad; but Mother was so nice that my sister told her all about the pretending game and the pussy cat, and Mother explained to her that you have to think even when you're pretending hard, and not do naughty things by mistake.

Then she told my sister all about why Mrs Lock was cross. About her rose-tree and the nasty thing that had happened to the smoky-looking cat. And my sister was very, very sorry.

When Mother went downstairs again my sister had a good idea. She went to her toy-box and she found the beautiful card that our granny had sent her for her birthday. It had a pretty picture of a pussy cat and a bunch of roses on it. It was the nicest card my sister had ever had, but she thought she would give it to Mrs Lock to show that she was sorry.

She didn't say a word to anyone. She went out very quietly down the road to Mrs Lock's gate.

When she got there, my little sister went inside the gate and up the path. The smoky-looking cat came round the side of the house to meet her, but she didn't stop to stroke him. No. She went up to Mrs Lock's front door, and rattled the letter box, then she pushed the postcard inside. She put her mouth close to the letter box and shouted, 'I am sorry I took your flower, Mrs Lock. I am very-very sorry. I have brought you my best postcard for a present.' And then she ran away again. Only this time Mrs Lock didn't tap the glass.

The very next time my little sister went by Mrs Lock's gate there was Mrs Lock herself, pulling weeds out of her pathway, and there was the smoky-looking cat sitting on a gatepost. When the cat saw my little sister he jumped down from the gatepost and said 'purr' to her and rubbed round and round her legs. Then Mrs Lock stood up very straight and looked over the gate at my little sister.

Mrs Lock said, 'Thank you for the card.'

All the time the smoky-coloured cat was purring and rubbing, rubbing and purring round and round my sister's legs and Mrs Lock said, 'My cat likes you. His name is Tibbles. Stroke him.'

And my sister did stroke him, and after that she stroked him every time she went past Mrs Lock's gate and found him sitting there in the sunshine. And although Mrs Lock often saw her stroking him she never said, 'Don't you meddle with my cat,' to her.

AND when Christmas-time came Mrs Lock sent my sister a card with robins and holly and shiny glittery stuff on it that was even more lovely than the pussy-cat card.

The naughtiest story of all

This is such a very terrible story about my naughty little sister that I hardly know how to tell it to you. It is all about one Christmas-time when I was a little girl, and my naughty little sister was a very little girl.

Now, my naughty little sister was very pleased when Christmas began to draw near, because she liked all the excitement of the plum-puddings and the turkeys, and the crackers and the holly, and all the Christmassy-looking shops, but there was one very awful thing about her – she didn't like to think about Father Christmas at all – she said he was a *horrid old man*!

There – I knew you would be shocked at that. But she did. And she said she wouldn't put up her stocking for him.

My mother told my naughty little sister what a good old man Father Christmas was, and how he brought the toys along on Christmas Eve, but my naughty little sister said, 'I don't care. And I don't want that nasty old man coming to our house.'

Well now, that was bad enough, wasn't it? But the really dreadful thing happened later on.

This is the dreadful thing: one day, my school-teacher said that a Father Christmas Man would be coming to the school to bring presents for all the children, and my teacher said that the Father Christmas Man would have toys for all our little brothers and sisters as well, if they cared to come along for them. She said that there would be a real Christmas tree with candles on it, and sweeties and cups of tea and biscuits for our mothers.

Wasn't that a nice thought? Well now, when I told my little sister about the Christmas tree, she said, 'Oh, nice!'

And when I told her about the sweeties she said, 'Very, very nice!' But when I told her about the Father Christmas Man, she said, 'Don't want *him*, nasty old man.'

Still, my mother said, 'You can't go to the Christmas tree without seeing him, so if you don't want to see him all that much, you will have to stay at home.'

But my naughty little sister did want to go, very much, so she said, 'I will go, and when the horrid Father Christmas Man comes in, I will close my eyes.'

So, we all went to the Christmas tree together, my mother and I, and my naughty little sister.

When we got to the school, my naughty little sister was very pleased to see all the pretty paper-chains that we had made in

school hung all round the classrooms, and when she saw all the little lanterns, and the holly and all the robin-redbreast drawings pinned on the blackboards she smiled and smiled. She was very smiley at first.

All the mothers, and the little brothers and sisters who were too young for school sat down on chairs and desks, and all the big school-children acted a play for them.

My little sister was very excited to see all the children dressed up as fairies and robins and elves and bo-peeps and things, and she clapped her hands very hard, like all the grown-ups did, to show that she was enjoying herself. And she still smiled.

Then, when some of the teachers came round with bags of sweets, tied up in pretty coloured paper, my little sister smiled even more, and she sang too when all the children sang. She sang, 'Away in a Manger', because she knew the words very well. When she didn't know the words of some of the singing, she 'la-la'd'.

After all the singing, the teachers put out the lights, and took away a big screen from a corner of the room, and there was the Christmas tree, all lit up with candles and shining with silvery stuff, and little shiny coloured balls. There were lots of toys on the tree, and all the children cheered and clapped.

Then the teachers put the lights on again, and blew out the candles, so that we could all go and look at the tree. My little sister went too. She looked at the tree, and she looked at the toys, and she saw a specially nice doll with a blue dress on, and she said, 'For me.'

My mother said, 'You must wait and see what you are given.'

Then the teachers called out, 'Back to your seats, everyone, we have a visitor coming.' So all the children went back to their seats, and sat still and waited and listened.

And, as we waited and listened, we heard a tinkle-tinkle bell noise, and then the schoolroom door opened, and in walked the Father Christmas Man. My naughty little sister had forgotten all about him, so she hadn't time to close her eyes before he walked in. However, when she saw him, my little sister stopped smiling and began to be stubborn.

The Father Christmas Man was very nice. He said he hoped we were having a good time, and we all said, 'Yes,' except my naughty little sister – she didn't say a thing.

Then he said, 'Now, one at a time, children; and I will give each one of you a toy.'

So, first of all each school-child went up for a toy, and my naughty little sister still didn't shut her eyes because she wanted to see who was going to have the specially nice doll in the blue dress. But none of the school-children had it.

Then Father Christmas began to call the little brothers and sisters up for presents, and, as he didn't know their names, he just said, 'Come along, sonny,' if it were a boy, and 'come along, girlie,' if it were a girl. The Father Christmas Man let the little brothers and sisters choose their own toys off the tree.

When my naughty little sister saw this, she was so worried about the specially nice doll, that she thought that she would just go up and get it. She said, 'I don't like that horrid old beardy man, but I do like that nice doll.'

So, my naughty little sister got up without being asked to, and she went right out to the front where the Father Christmas Man was standing, and she said, 'That doll, please,' and pointed to the doll she wanted.

The Father Christmas Man laughed and all the teachers laughed, and the other mothers and the school-children, and all the little brothers and sisters. My mother did not laugh because she was so shocked to see my naughty little sister going out without being asked to.

The Father Christmas Man took the specially nice doll off the tree, and he handed it to my naughty little sister and he said, 'Well now, I hear you don't like me very much, but won't you just shake hands?'

and my naughty little sister said, 'No.' But she
took the doll all the same.

The Father Christmas Man put out
his nice old hand for her to shake and
be friends, and do you know what that
naughty bad girl did? *She bit his hand.* She
really and truly did. Can you think of anything more dreadful and
terrible? She bit Father Christmas's good old hand, and then she
turned and ran and ran out of the school with all the children staring
after her, and her doll held very tight in her arms.

The Father Christmas Man was very nice, he said it wasn't a
hard bite, only a frightened one, and he made all the children
sing songs together.

When my naughty little sister was brought back by my mother,
she said she was very sorry, and the Father Christmas Man said,
'That's all right, old lady,' and because he was so smiley and nice
to her, my funny little sister went right up to him, and gave him
a big 'sorry' kiss, which pleased him very much.

And she hung her stocking up after all, and that kind man
remembered to fill it for her.

My naughty little sister kept the specially nice doll until she was
quite grown-up. She called it Rosy-Primrose, and although she was
sometimes bad-tempered with it, she really loved it very much indeed.